Marvels & Mysteries by Richard Marsh

Richard Bernard Heldmann was born on 12th October 1857, in St Johns Wood, North London.

By his early 20's Heldmann began publishing fiction for the myriad magazine publications that had sprung up and were eager for good well-written content.

In October 1882, Heldmann was promoted to co-editor of Union Jack, a popular magazine, but his association with the publication ended suddenly in June 1883. It appears Heldman was prone to issuing forged cheques to finance his lifestyle. In April 1884 He was sentenced to 18 months hard labour.

In order to be well away from the scandal and damage this had caused to his reputation Heldmann adopted a pseudonym on his release from jail. Shortly thereafter the name 'Richard Marsh' began to appear in the literary periodicals. The use of his mother's maiden name as part of it seems both a release and a lifeline.

A stroke of very good fortune arrived with his novel The Beetle published in 1897. This would turn out to be his greatest commercial success and added some much-needed gravitas to his literary reputation.

Marsh was a prolific writer and wrote almost 80 volumes of fiction as well as many short stories, across many genres from horror and crime to romance and humour.

Index of Contents

The Long Arm of Coincidence

I. The Portmanteau

Mr. Bidder had a telegram in his hand. Here it is:

"Come up at once. Stone, Scotland Yard"

Mr. Bidder was the senior partner in the firm of Bidder, Tuxwell, and Harris, of Birkenhead. A confidential clerk one Raymond Hastie had been discovered in an extensive system of embezzlement. Mr. Hastie had disappeared, and with him some necessary books and a considerable sum in cash as well. The affair was in the hands of the police, and the above curt telegram had been just received from that well-known officer, George Stone, of Scotland Yard.

Mr. Bidder left for London almost immediately after its receipt. He journeyed by the train which leaves Liverpool at 4.5 p.m, and is due at Euston at half-past eight. He took with him a black portmanteau. It was one of tolerable size. He was a spruce gentleman, and as he might be detained in town for a day or two he thought it would be as well to go provided.

In his first-class compartment there was but one other passenger. This was a slight, weedy-looking gentleman, who was enveloped in a voluminous overcoat which was obviously not of English manufacture. The afternoon was dull, there was more than a suspicion of mist in the air; but though it was cool, it was still not cold enough for the average Britisher to sit muffled to the chin in a curiously shaped garment made of Irish frieze, apparently about an inch in thickness. Mr. Bidder eyed his fellow-passenger, though there was not much of him to be seen; for, in addition to being muffled to the chin, he wore a soft felt hat which he had pulled down to his eyes. Mr. Bidder was conversationally inclined, but he felt persuaded that there was little in the shape of social intercourse to be got out of the gentleman who crouched at the other end of the carriage. Still he thought he would try.

"Going through?"

Mr. Bidder flattered himself that the tone in which he put this inquiry was genial. But the fact is, he was used to public speaking of a kind—teetotal and down-with-everything-pleasant platforms, and such like—and in spite of himself his manner was pompous, and, perhaps, a trifle dictatorial. Still, this was not sufficient to account for the behaviour of the gentleman addressed. That individual sprang from his seat and turned towards Mr. Bidder with a gesture which was distinctly threatening. For a moment it really appeared as though he was about to assault him. If such was his intention he very wisely thought better of it, and sank back into his corner.

"What's that to do with you?" he growled.

Mr. Bidder was conscious that it had nothing to do with him; still, the fact might have been stated in more courteous fashion. He began to consider whether it would not be advisable at the first stopping station to get into another carriage. But when they did stop other passengers got in who appeared to be quite as much disposed to talk as he was.

At Euston, in connection with this gentleman, something really remarkable happened. Mr. Bidder was going along the platform in search of his portmanteau when he met a porter bearing the identical article aloft upon his shoulder. By his side walked the gentleman in the overcoat. Mr. Bidder stopped.

"Porter, that's my portmanteau! What do you mean by walking off with it?"

The porter seemed to be a little surprised.

"Yours? Why, this gentleman says it's 'is."

"It is nothing of the kind. Take it to my cab. It's mine!"

"Yours!" The gentleman in the overcoat stepped in front of him. He seemed to be literally shaking with rage. "If you don't stow that I'll make you sit up sharp. Give me that portmanteau!"

He stretched out his hand to take the portmanteau from the porter; but Mr. Bidder was not to be bullied out of his property quite so easily as that.

"You will do nothing of the kind, porter. I tell you that portmanteau's mine. Call a constable. Officer!"

There was a policeman standing a little distance off. Mr. Bidder beckoned to him. Directly he did so the stranger's face assumed a peculiarly ghastly hue. Without a word he slunk off and disappeared in the crowd.

The porter was amazed.

"Well, that beats anything. That's the coolest hand I ever see. He came to me and says, 'Put that portmanteau on a cab,' as though he was a dook. Are you going to give him in charge?"

"I ought to, but I'm in a hurry. I'll let the scoundrel go scot free this time."

Off went Mr. Bidder in triumph with the porter and portmanteau. He told the cab-man to drive to a certain well-known hotel. When he reached it a man suddenly appeared at the side of the cab and looked at him. Mr. Bidder stared in return, for the man was a perfect stranger. He was one of the tallest men he had ever seen, six foot five or six, with a moustache of the most extravagant dimensions. The hotel porter coming to take the luggage from the driver, the man stood aside on the pavement. But as he went up the steps Mr. Bidder not only saw the fellow wink at him, but even hook his finger on to the bridge of his nose with a gesture which was not only familiar but impertinent. Mr. Bidder, who had not yet altogether recovered from his adventure with the gentleman in the overcoat, told himself that the man was drunk.

It was considerably past nine o'clock. Mr. Bidder was hungry. Giving instructions to have some dinner prepared for him, Mr. Bidder followed his portmanteau to his bedroom. The hotel porter having removed the strap, all he had to do was to insert the key and turn the lock. But this was exactly what he was unable to do. There was something the matter either with the key or the lock, for the key would not turn. Mr. Bidder began to lose his temper. It was long past his regular dinner-hour, and he was very hungry indeed. He examined the key; it seemed to be all right. He put it again into the lock; but no, it would not turn.

"I wonder if that scamp has been playing any tricks with the lock?"

He alluded to the gentleman in the overcoat; but a moment's reflection showed him that that was scarcely possible. He had seen the portmanteau put into the luggage-van with his own eyes; it had reposed in the luggage-van throughout the journey; certainly the gentleman in the overcoat had not stirred from his own corner of the carriage. On their arrival scarcely a moment had elapsed before he had detected the enterprising traveller in the act of escorting his prize. It was impossible that it could have been tampered with by him.

Mr. Bidder tried again. He gave the key an extra twist: it turned—indeed, it turned with a vengeance. But that was not the only cause which induced him to so precipitately assume an upright position on his feet. It was perhaps a little surprising that the key should all at once have turned so readily, but it was much more surprising that, simultaneously, such a peculiar sound should have begun to issue from what might, metaphorically, be called the bosom of the portmanteau, and not only begun, but continued—in fact, was continuing as Mr. Bidder stared down at the receptacle of his belongings.

"Whatever have I put inside to make such a noise as that?"

He knelt down to see, but the portmanteau refused to open. The key was still in the lock. He felt quite sure he had turned it; still, he might be mistaken, so he made another trial. Whether he had or had not turned it before, it turned quite easily again, and instantly the noise redoubled. The thing might have been alive, and resenting the touch of its owner's hand. Mr. Bidder sprang to his feet again; he was not only surprised, he was even startled.

"It sounds exactly as though someone had set the mechanism of some clockwork going. Good—" He hesitated before he let the word come out, but it did come out. "Good heavens! I don't believe that after all the thing is mine."

By "the thing" he meant the portmanteau. When the thought first struck him the perspiration stood upon his brow. Was he the thief? Had he robbed that other man? What a barefaced scoundrel the gentleman in the overcoat must have taken him to be! The idea was horrible, but close examination showed that it was true: the portmanteau was not his. It bore a strong superficial resemblance to the genuine article, but none the less it was not the real thing. It is not difficult, especially at night, to mistake one portmanteau for another—a fact which was acutely realised by Mr. Bidder then. He was aghast. He was a man of some imagination, and a mental picture was present to his mind—what must the gentleman in the overcoat be thinking of him then? And he had beckoned to a policeman too!

As he was still trying to realise the situation someone tried the handle of the bedroom door, and, finding it locked, tapped at the panel. Mr. Bidder opened. A stout, middle-aged man immediately stepped inside and closed the door behind him.

"I'm a detective."

"A detective!" cried Mr. Bidder, his brain in a whirl. "The very man I want."

"Indeed," rejoined the newcomer with a noticeable dryness. "That's odd, because you're the very man I'm wanting too."

Mr. Bidder was the very man he wanted! A detective!

Was it possible that the gentleman in the overcoat had already laid information, and he was actually suspected of crime? The situation was distinctly not a nice one, but it was obvious that it only required a few words of explanation.

"It is absurd; one of the most absurd things of which I ever heard, though I own that at first sight it must have a suspicious appearance to a stranger's eye."

Mr. Bidder laughed uneasily; he was scarcely in a jovial frame of mind.

"I suppose you know what I want you for?"

"I suppose I do if you put it in that uncomfortable sort of way. But, my dear sir, if you will allow me to explain—"

"You can make a statement at your own risk, and I shall take it down. But perhaps first you'd better hear the warrant read."

"The warrant!" Mr. Bidder stared.

"The warrant."

"You don't mean to say there has been a warrant taken out already?"

"I don't know what you call already. The warrant has been out three months."

"Three months! Why, the thing has only just occurred!"

The detective gave quite a start.

"You don't mean to say you've been up to any of your tricks already?"

"My tricks, sir! What on earth do you mean?"

"I don't want to have any talk with you. We expected you over three months ago; we're not so fast asleep as some of you fellows seem to think. I don't know how it was I missed you at Liverpool, but I was on your track directly afterwards, and you only slipped me at Euston by the skin of your teeth."

By this time it began to dawn upon Mr. Bidder that a certain amount of confusion existed either in his or in the detective's mind.

"Will you be so good as to tell me who and what you take me for?"

"I'm going to arrest you on the charge of bringing over an infernal machine from America to England."

"An infernal machine!" gasped Mr. Bidder.

"From information received, I believe the thing is called a dynamite portmanteau."

"A dynamite portmanteau!" Mr. Bidder turned to the portmanteau on the floor. "You don't mean to say that this—that that fellow's portmanteau— Good heavens! you don't mean to say that this apparently innocent-looking piece of luggage is a dynamite portmanteau?"

"Is that the article? What's that noise?"

"It's—it's the portmanteau."

"You infernal villain! you don't mean that you've set it going?"

The detective made a bolt for the door, dragging Mr. Bidder with him. He flung it open, but he was just too late to get outside, for there was a vivid flame, a blinding smoke, a loud report, and the next thing Mr. Bidder and the detective were conscious of was that they were lying on the top of the landing in the centre of a crowd of excited people.

"They're not dead," said someone.

"Nor likely to die!" exclaimed a voice at Mr. Bidder's side, and the detective staggered to his feet. Mr. Bidder felt that he would rather lie a little longer where he was. The detective pulled himself together.

"I'm a detective. There's been an explosion. This man has tried to blow the place up with an infernal machine."

"I protest!" cried Mr. Bidder, struggling to stand up straight to deny the charge. The detective, thrusting his fingers into the collar of his shirt so as to almost choke him, nipped his denial in the bud.

"Are there any constables here?"

"Heaps," replied one of the bystanders. "The house is full of them, and the street as well."

As a matter of fact a couple of constables immediately advanced.

"You know me?"

"You're Mr. Humes, sir. We know you very well."

"Is there an inspector here?"

"Inspector, sir, is downstairs."

"I'll go down to him. See that no one goes inside that room; for all I know, there may be another explosion still to come."

Mr. Humes went down; Mr. Bidder went with him—with Mr. Humes' fingers in his collar. In the hall they encountered an inspector. The trio adjourned to a little room upon one side. Here they were immediately joined by the manager of the hotel.

"What is the meaning of this?" inquired that gentleman.

"It means that this man has brought an infernal machine over from America and exploded it in your hotel."

"It is false!" gasped Mr. Bidder. "Officer, I insist upon you taking your hand away from my throat."

Mr. Humes nodded to the inspector; the inspector approached, his hands to his pocket. In an instant Mr. Bidder had a pair of handcuffs on his wrists. Then Mr. Humes removed his fingers.

Mr. Bidder was almost inarticulate with rage. He put great pressure on himself in order to retain a degree of self-control.

"You are making a hideous mistake. I tell you I know no more about what has occurred than you do."

"I suppose the thing went off before you meant it to; and that you didn't intend to be right on top of it when it did go off I can easily believe."

Mr. Humes smiled at his auditors.

"The thing went off before I meant it to! I am James Bidder, of the firm of Bidder, Tuxwell, and Harris, of Birkenhead. If you will let me get at my pockets I will give you proof of every word I say."

"You can do that equally well at the station," said Mr. Humes.

"You had better take him the back way," suggested the inspector. "There's an ugly crowd in front:"—he pointedly addressed himself to Mr. Bidder—"if they got hold of you they might tear you to pieces."

"Tear me to pieces!"

"Dynamite's not popular in an English crowd."

"But, my dear sir, I tell you that the whole thing—"

"Come along; we've had enough of that." Mr. Humes opened the door. He spoke to the constable without. "Get me a cab round at the back."

"There's one, sir, waiting for you already."

"All right. Come along now." Mr. Bidder went along, escorted by the guardians of the law. It seemed to him that he was in a dream. He was too bewildered to be entirely master of his thoughts, but a hazy idea presented itself to his mind—what a subject to ventilate in the Times! He would have deemed it incredible that any respectable man, entirely innocent of anything but a deep-rooted abhorrence of any sort of crime, could have been subjected to the indignities which were being heaped upon him then. When they reached the door they found that a hansom cab was waiting them in the street. It was a little narrow street, not too well lighted. There were a few loiterers about, but nothing in the shape of an ugly crowd. When Mr. Humes saw it was a hansom he drew back.

"Why didn't you get a four-wheeler?" he asked.

"There wasn't one to be had."

Without another word the detective hurried Mr. Bidder across the little strip of pavement. When they were seated he gave the direction to the driver, "Bow Street Police Station," and the cab was off.

"If anyone had told me," said Mr. Bidder, who found it impossible to keep still, "that a person in my position could have been the victim of such a blunder as this, I should have been prepared to stake all that I possess in the world on the fact that the man was lying."

"That's right. Pitch a yarn or two, only don't throw them away on me."

"A dynamite portmanteau!"

"Just so—a dynamite portmanteau."

"I never heard of such a thing."

"I don't suppose you ever did."

"What we hear about the blunders of the foreign police is nothing compared to this."

"I daresay you know more about the foreign police than I do."

"Sir!"

"Now, then, sit still. Stow that! What on earth— Driver!"

To this day Mr. Bidder does not know exactly what it was that happened. They were going up a narrow, ill-lighted street; suddenly someone sprang off the pavement and leaped at the horse's head; this person was followed by others, dark figures seen dimly in the night. They did something to the horse; the animal swerved violently to one side; the hansom was overturned. Mr. Bidder was conscious that it fell on one side, with him inside it, then consciousness forsook him.

II. The Portmanteau's Friends

When Mr. Bidder regained consciousness he was lying on a sofa. The room was strange. It was a small, ill-furnished room, lighted by a common oil-lamp, which stood on a small square table, which was covered by a gaudy green tablecloth. A man was bending over him. When this person perceived signs of reviving, he announced the fact aloud.

"He's coming to. How are you feeling now?"

"Thank you, I—I'm feeling rather queer."

"I guess you oughter."

The man was smiling down at him. He was a big, stout man, with profuse red hair and whiskers. He spoke with that curious twang which we associate with that latest example of cross-breeding in races, the Irish-American.

"Where am I?" inquired Mr. Bidder.

"You're here, that's where you are. And you're safe along with us."

Mr. Bidder sat up on the couch. He then perceived that his companion and he were not alone; three other men were in the room. Mr. Bidder stared at them, and they stared at him, then they exchanged a curious glance. Mr. Bidder put his hand up to his forehead, feeling as though he were seeing things happen in a dream. The red-haired man went on—

"Didn't I do it neat?"

"Do what neat?"

"Bust up that one-horse show."

"I'm afraid I don't quite understand you."

"When we heard that you were nicked, I said to the boys, 'The only thing we can do is to spoil the procession.' So I kinder stood the cab on its head."

Mr. Bidder stared at the speaker with all his eyes.

"You don't mean that you upset the cab on purpose?"

"I guess I did. Very much on purpose too."

"Good heavens! You might have killed me."

"That is so. It was kill or cure. We ran for cure, and scooped the pool."

Mr. Bidder continued to stare with bewildered eyes.

"May I ask what interest you took in me, a perfect stranger, which could justify you in precipitating me from a hansom cab which was going at full speed through the public streets?"

The red-haired man laughed; the three other men laughed too. One of them came and stood in front of Mr. Bidder. He was a man of gigantic stature, and wore a moustache of quite preposterous dimensions, one of those moustaches which burlesque villains wear upon the stage. Mr. Bidder thought that he had seen that gentleman before. The man hooked his finger on to his nose; then Mr. Bidder knew he had. It was the man who had stared into the cab on his arrival at the "Golden Cross Hotel."

"Castle Garden," said the man, still with his finger on the bridge of his nose.

"I beg your pardon."

"Castle Garden," repeated the man.

Mr. Bidder stared about him, feeling that these things must be taking place in a dream.

"What about Castle Garden?" he murmured, as though he were playing a game of questions and answers.

"Have they changed the countersign?" asked a slight, dark-faced man who was standing at Mr. Bidder's back.

"The countersign? I don't understand."

The red-haired man spoke next.

"You're cautious, but don't you think you carry it a bit too far? We're safe."

Mr. Bidder stood up. He let his eyes travel slowly round the room. Then he eyed each of the four men; they were strangers to him.

"There is some hideous mistake! Where am I? Is this a lunatic asylum?"

A distinct pause followed this remark.

"A lunatic asylum!" exclaimed the dark-faced man.

"It can't be a room in a gaol!" repeated the previous speaker.

Suddenly the giant with the preposterous moustache laid his great hand on Mr. Bidder's shoulder, and, bending down, looked closely into his face.

"Who are you? Aren't you the Scorcher?"

"The Scorcher?" Was the man a lunatic? "The Scorcher? I'm James Bidder!"

"And who in thunder is James Bidder?"

"Well," replied the owner of the name in his perplexity, "I'm beginning myself to wonder who he is."

The fourth man, who had not yet taken part in the discussion, interposed. He was a little, wiry man, with an excited manner.

"See here, let's see this hand. Did you bring over that portmanteau, or didn't you?"

"Portmanteau! What portmanteau?"

"That dynamite affair."

"Upon my faith as a Christian, and my honour as a man, I know nothing of the thing."

The language was melodramatic, but its result was effective. The countenances of Mr. Bidder's four listeners perceptibly changed.

"You're not playing it off on us?"

"I don't know what you mean. I tell you there's some hideous mistake. I don't know who you are and where I am. Who are you?"

"I reckon we'll know who you are, anyhow." The wiry man went to the door, locked it, and slipped the key into his pocket. "General, let's see his papers."

The big man seized him by the shoulder.

"Shell out!" he said.

"What do you mean?"

"Empty your pockets upon that table."

"Are you going to rob me?"

"We are not. We are going to conduct a little inquiry. There has been a slight mistake made somewhere, and we're going to ascertain where it just comes in."

Perceiving that resistance would be useless, Mr. Bidder emptied the contents of his pockets out upon the table. The big man took up his pocket-book; from it he took a slip of paper. It was the telegram in which Mr. Stone had summoned Mr. Bidder up to town. Directly the big man read it his hands dropped to his side.

"Good God! we're sold!" he cried.

There was silence. In the silence Mr. Bidder became conscious that each of the four was holding a revolver in his hand.

"What do you mean?" asked the red-haired man.

"It's a plant! We've given ourselves away! He's a spy—that's what our friend here is. Here's a telegram from Stone at the Yard, instructing him to come up at once to town. If you move, or open your lips to give a sign to your friends outside, you're gone!"

The big man raised his revolver—and pointed it at Mr. Bidder. Mr. Bidder had read in books of such things happening, but he had never realised the possibility of the muzzle of a six-shooter being within six inches of his head, and that in the London of today.

"You—you wrong me," he stammered; "you—misjudge me. You misconstrue the telegram entirely."

"Do we? We'll misconstrue you if you don't dry up. How much do you know?"

"Know? Nothing!"

"Don't try that barney on with us. Tell us straight out how much you know, or you'll know everything— on the other side."

"But I assure you that the whole thing, from first to last, has been a chapter of accidents. First the police mistook me for somebody else, and now, apparently, you are making the same mistake as the police."

The four men listened. Perceiving that he was being listened to, Mr. Bidder, gathering courage, did his best to throw some light upon the subject.

"I am James Bidder, of the firm of Bidder, Tuxwell, and Harris. If you will examine those papers you will find that is so. A clerk, a man named Hastie, has been defrauding us of a large sum of money. The case is in the hands of the police. With reference to it this morning I received that telegram, which brought me up to town. At Euston I thought I saw a man walking off with my portmanteau. I threatened to give him into custody. He immediately slunk off, leaving the portmanteau with me. I took it with me to the hotel."

"I saw your arrival," the giant said.

"I know you did. I didn't know who you were from Adam then, and I don't know who you are from Adam now."

"Go on," said the red-haired man. "This tale is getting funny."

"When I began to unlock the portmanteau, I found that it wasn't mine. It could be easily mistaken for mine, and I had mistaken it. In trying to unlock it I seemed to have set some sort of internal machinery in motion." The red-haired man chuckled. "While I was wondering what the noise could be, and what I had better do, the door opened and a man came in. When he said that he was a detective, and that he wanted me, I immediately jumped to the conclusion that it was for the theft of the portmanteau." The red-haired man burst into a roar. His friends were smiling. "When he said it was for bringing over an infernal machine from America, I thought that he was mad. While I was endeavouring to explain the mistake that he had made, there was an explosion."

"From the portmanteau?"

"From the portmanteau—at least, I suppose it was."

"Did it do much damage?"

"That I cannot say. We did not stay in the room to make inquiries. We fell over each other on the landing. In spite of all that I could say, that idiot of a detective persisted in taking me to the station. While I was still remonstrating with him in the cab, according to your own account, you appeared and turned it over."

"We mistook you for a friend of ours," observed the red-haired man.

"It was very kind of you, I'm sure." Mr. Bidder's tone was rueful. "Gentlemen, if you will examine those papers which are lying on the table, you will find that the account I have given of myself is the correct one."

They examined the papers, whispering among themselves as they did so. Then the big man turned to Mr. Bidder.

"Mr. Bidder, there is only one part of this unfortunate business on which we can congratulate ourselves—that it has given us the pleasure of your acquaintance."

"Don't mention it," said Mr. Bidder with a groan.

"We were expecting a friend from America. He was, personally, a stranger to us, but he was to travel to London by the same train by which you travelled. He was to bring a black portmanteau, and he was to go to the 'Golden Cross Hotel.' When I saw you turn up there to time, with the black portmanteau outside your cab, I took it for granted you were he; when we heard that you were in the hands of the police we concluded that the best service we could render you would be to stop the show."

"I understand exactly."

"We are not going to ask you to make any promise not to endanger our liberty by revealing what has taken place this night. We are going to put it out of your power to do so." Mr. Bidder started. "No, we are not going to murder you; we are going to ask you to drink this."

The big man produced from his waistcoat pocket a small phial containing a colourless liquid.

"What is it? Poison?"

"Not poison. It is a drug which will stupefy you for the next four-and-twenty hours. By that time we shall be out of danger, and you can tell what tales you please."

"What? Good heavens! Do you ask me to drink, of my own free will, stuff which will make a dead man of me for at least the next four-and-twenty hours, perhaps never to rally again?"

"As it is a matter in which time presses, we must trouble you to drink it now. It is, you understand, a case of necessity. It is either this or this."

The big man handled his revolver, suggesting that the choice lay between that and the contents of the phial.

"But, my dear sir, I assure you—"

"You need not. Remonstrances are thrown away on us as on the detective."

"Was ever a man of my commercial, moral, and social standing placed in such a position before? I do beg of you—"

"Which is it to be?"

"Which is it to be?"

The big man brought his revolver breast high. Mr. Bidder saw that the others were raising their revolvers too.

"Give me the phial!"

It was given him. Drawing the cork he sniffed at the contents.

"Quickly, please."

Mr. Bidder saw that the men were closing in. He put the phial to his lips, and drained its contents to the dregs.

When Mr. Bidder again regained consciousness—for the second time—he was lying under a railway arch at Parson's Green. He was unable to give any account of how he arrived at that somewhat remote district of London. A railway porter found him just as he was regaining consciousness. His watch, chain, money, and papers were in his pockets, even the telegram which had summoned him to town—nothing was gone. He went immediately to the local police-station, thence to headquarters, and at both places he told his tale. It created some sensation, but the rogues were never caught; the affair of the dynamite portmanteau is to this day a mystery.

All this happened some time ago, when dynamite was in the air. A year or two afterwards, Mr. Bidder, who happened to be spending a few days in town, relaxed his rule so far as actually to go and see a play. The hero made some allusion to the "long arm of coincidence"; critics said that that long arm of coincidence was about as much as they could swallow. That same night, when the play was over, Mr. Bidder made the present writer his confidant, telling him the tale which now is told, prefacing it with the remark—

"Talk about the long arm of coincidence, what do you call this?"

I told him when the narration was finished that I called it a case of the "long arm of coincidence" too.

The Mask

I. What Happened in the Train

"Wigmakers have brought their art to such perfection that it is difficult to detect false hair from real. Why should not the same skill be shown in the manufacture of a mask? Our faces, in one sense, are nothing but masks. Why should not the imitation be as good as the reality? Why, for instance, should not this face of mine, as you see it, be nothing but a mask—a something which I can take off and on?"

She laid her two hands softly against her cheeks. There was a ring of laughter in her voice.

"Such a mask would not only be, in the highest sense, a work of art, but it would also be a thing of beauty—a joy for ever."

"You think that I am beautiful?"

I could not doubt it—with her velvet skin just tinted with the bloom of health, her little dimpled chin, her ripe red lips, her flashing teeth, her great, inscrutable dark eyes, her wealth of hair which gleamed in the sun-light. I told her so.

"So you think that I am beautiful? How odd—how very odd!"

I could not tell if she was in jest or earnest. Her lips were parted by a smile. But it did not seem to me that it was laughter which was in her eyes.

"And you have only seen me, for the first time, a few hours ago?"

"Such has been my ill-fortune."

She rose. She stood for a moment looking down at me.

"And you think there is nothing in my theory about—a mask?"

"On the contrary, I think there is a great deal in any theory you may advance."

A waiter brought me a card on a salver.

"Gentleman wishes to see you, sir."

I glanced at the card. On it was printed, "George Davis, Scotland Yard." As I was looking at the piece of pasteboard she passed behind me.

"Perhaps I shall see you again, when we will continue our discussion about—a mask."

I rose and bowed. She went from the verandah down the steps into the garden.

I turned to the waiter. "Who is that lady?"

"I don't know her name, sir. She came in last night. She has a private sitting-room at No. 22." He hesitated. Then he added, "I'm not sure, sir, but I think the lady's name is Jaynes—Mrs. Jaynes."

"Where is Mr. Davis? Show him into my room."

I went to my room and awaited him. Mr. Davis proved to be a short, spare man, with iron-grey whiskers and a quiet, unassuming manner.

"You had my telegram, Mr. Davis?"

"We had, sir."

"I believe you are not unacquainted with my name?"

"Know it very well, sir."

"The circumstances of my case are so peculiar, Mr. Davis, that, instead of going to the local police, I thought it better to at once place myself in communication with headquarters." Mr. Davis bowed. "I came down yesterday afternoon by the express from Paddington. I was alone in a first-class carriage. At Swindon a young gentle-man got in. He seemed to me to be about twenty-three or four years of age, and unmistakably a gentleman. We had some conversation together. At Bath he offered me a drink out of his flask. It was getting evening then. I have been hard at it for the last few weeks. I was tired. I suppose I fell asleep. In my sleep I dreamed."

"You dreamed?"

"I dreamed that I was being robbed." The detective smiled. "As you surmise, I woke up to find that my dream was real. But the curious part of the matter is that I am unable to tell you where my dream ended, and where my wakefulness began. I dreamed that something was leaning over me, rifling my person—some hideous, gasping thing which, in its eagerness, kept emitting short cries which were of the nature of barks. Although I say I dreamed this, I am not at all sure I did not actually see it taking place. The purse was drawn from my trousers pocket; something was taken out of it. I distinctly heard the chink of money, and then the purse was returned to where it was before. My watch and chain were taken, the studs out of my shirt, the links out of my wrist-bands. My pocket-book was treated as my purse had been—something was taken out of it and the book returned. My keys were taken. My dressing bag was taken from the rack, opened, and articles were taken out of it, though I could not see what articles they were. The bag was replaced on the rack, the keys in my pocket."

"Didn't you see the face of the person who did all this?"

"That was the curious part of it. I tried to, but I failed. It seemed to me that the face was hidden by a veil."

"The thing was simple enough. We shall have to look for your young gentleman friend."

"Wait till I have finished. The thing—I say the thing because, in my dream, I was strongly, nay, horribly under the impression that I was at the mercy of some sort of animal, some creature of the ape or monkey tribe."

"There, certainly, you dreamed."

"You think so? Still, wait a moment. The thing, whatever it was, when it had robbed me, opened my shirt at the breast, and, deliberately tearing my skin with what seemed to me to be talons, put its mouth to the wound, and, gathering my flesh between its teeth, bit me to the bone. Here is sufficient evidence to prove that then, at least, I did not dream."

Unbuttoning my shirt I showed Mr. Davis the open cicatrice.

"The pain was so intense that it awoke me. I sprang to my feet. I saw the thing."

"You saw it?"

"I saw it. It was crouching at the other end of the carriage. The door was open. I saw it for an instant as it leaped into the night."

"At what rate do you suppose the train was travelling?"

"The carriage blinds were drawn. The train had just left Newton Abbot. The creature must have been biting me when the train was actually drawn up at the platform. It leaped out of the carriage as the train was restarting."

"And did you see the face?"

"I did. It was the face of a devil."

"Excuse me, Mr. Fountain, but you're not trying on me the plot of your next novel—just to see how it goes?"

"I wish I were, my lad, but I am not. It was the face of a devil—so hideous a face that the only detail I was able to grasp was that it had a pair of eyes which gleamed at me like burning coals."

"Where was the young gentleman?"

"He had disappeared."

"Precisely. And I suppose you did not only dream you had been robbed?"

"I had been robbed of everything which was of the slightest value, except eighteen shillings. Exactly that sum had been left in my purse."

"Now perhaps you will give me a description of the young gentleman and his flask."

"I swear it was not he who robbed me."

"The possibility is that he was disguised. To my eye it seems unreasonable to suppose that he should have removed his disguise while engaged in the very act of robbing you. Anyhow, you give me his description, and I shouldn't be surprised if I was able to lay my finger on him on the spot."

I described him—the well-knit young man, with his merry eyes, his slight moustache, his graceful manners.

"If he was a thief, then I am no judge of character. There was something about him which, to my eyes, marked him as emphatically a gentleman."

The detective only smiled,

"The first thing I shall have to do will be to telegraph all over the country a list of the stolen property. Then I may possibly treat myself to a little private think. Your story is rather a curious one, Mr. Fountain. And then later in the day I may want to say a word or two with you again. I shall find you here?"

I said that he would. When he had gone I sat down and wrote a letter. When I had finished the letter I went along the corridor towards the front door of the hotel. As I was going I saw in front of me a figure—the figure of a man. He was standing still, and his back was turned my way. But something about him struck me with such a sudden force of recognition that, stopping short, I stared. I suppose I must, unconsciously, have uttered some sort of exclamation, because the instant I stopped short, with a quick movement, he wheeled right round. We faced each other.

"You!" I exclaimed.

I hurried forward with a cry of recognition. He advanced, as I thought, to greet me. But he had only taken a step or two in my direction when he turned into a room upon his right, and, shutting the door behind him, disappeared.

"The man in the train!" I told myself.

If I had had any doubt upon the subject his sudden disappearance would have cleared my doubt away. If he was anxious to avoid a meeting with me, all the more reason why I should seek an interview with him. I went to the door of the room which he had entered and, without the slightest hesitation, I turned the handle. The room was empty—there could be no doubt of that. It was an ordinary hotel sitting-room, own brother to the one which I occupied myself, and, as I saw at a glance, contained no article of furniture behind which a person could be concealed. But at the other side of the room was another door.

"My gentleman," I said, "has gone through that."

Crossing the room again I turned the handle. This time without result the door was locked. I rapped against the panels. Instantly someone addressed me from within.

"Who's that?"

The voice, to my surprise, and also somewhat to my discomfiture, was a woman's.

"Excuse me, but might I say one word to the gentleman who has just entered the room?"

"What's that? Who are you?"

"I'm the gentleman who came down with him in the train."

"What?"

The door opened. A woman appeared—the lady whom the waiter had said he believed was a Mrs. Jaynes, and who had advanced that curious story about a mask being made to imitate the human face. She had a dressing jacket on, and her glorious hair was flowing loose over her shoulders. I was so surprised to see her that for a moment I was tongue-tied. The surprise seemed to be mutual, for, with a pretty air of bewilderment, stepping back into the room she partially closed the door.

"I thought it was the waiter. May I ask, sir, what it is you want?"

"I beg ten thousand pardons; but might I just have one word with your husband?"

"With whom, sir?"

"Your husband."

"My husband?"

Again throwing the door wide open she stood and stared at me.

"I refer, madam, to the gentleman whom I just saw enter the room."

"I don't know if you intend an impertinence, sir, or merely a jest."

Her lip curled, her eyes flashed—it was plain she was offended.

"I just saw, madam, in the corridor a gentleman with whom I travelled yesterday from London. I advanced to meet him. As I did so he turned into your sitting-room. When I followed him I found it empty, so I took it for granted he had come in here."

"You are mistaken, sir. I know no gentleman in the hotel. As for my husband, my husband has been dead three years."

I could not contradict her, yet it was certain I had seen the stranger turn into the outer room. I told her so.

"If any man entered my sitting-room—which was an unwarrantable liberty to take—he must be in it now. Except yourself, no one has come near my bedroom. I have had the door locked, and, as you see, I have been dressing. Are you sure you have not been dreaming?"

If I had been dreaming I had been dreaming with my eyes open; and yet, if I had seen the man enter the room—and I could have sworn I had—where was he now? She offered, with scathing irony, to let me examine her own apartment. Indeed, she opened the door so wide that I could see all over it from where I stood. It was plain enough that, with the exception of herself, it had no occupant.

And yet, I asked myself, as I retreated with my tail a little between my legs, how could I have been mistaken? The only hypothesis I could hit upon was, that my thoughts had been so deeply engaged upon the matter that they had made me the victim of hallucination. Perhaps my nervous system had temporarily been disorganised by my misadventures of the day before. And yet—and this was the final conclusion to which I came upon the matter if I had not seen my fellow-passenger standing in front of me, a creature of flesh and blood, I would never trust the evidence of my eyes again. The most ardent ghost-seer never saw a ghost in the middle of the day.

I went for a walk towards Babbicombe. My nerves might be a little out of order—though not to the extent of seeing things which were non-existent, and it was quite possible that fresh air and exercise might do them good. I lunched at Babbicombe, spending the afternoon, as the weather was so fine, upon the seashore, in company with my thoughts, my pipe, and a book. But as the day wore on a sea mist stole over the land, and as I returned Torquaywards it was already growing dusk. I went back by way of the sea-front. As I was passing Hesketh Crescent I stood for a moment looking out into the gloom which was gathering over the sea. As I looked I heard, or I thought that I heard, a sound just behind me. As I heard it the blood seemed to run cold in my veins, and I had to clutch at the coping of the sea-wall to prevent my knees from giving way under me. It was the sound which I had heard in my dream in the train, and which had seemed to come from the creature which was robbing me: the cry or bark of some wild beast. It came once, one short, quick, gasping bark, then all was still. I looked round, fearing to see I know not what. Nothing was in sight. Yet, although nothing could be seen, I felt that there was something there. But, as the silence continued, I began to laugh at myself beneath my breath. I had not supposed that I was such a coward as to be frightened at less than a shadow! Moving away from the walk, I was about to resume my walk, when it came again—the choking, breathless bark so close to me that I seemed to feel the warm breath upon my cheek. Looking swiftly round, I saw, almost touching mine, the face of the creature which I had seen, but only for an instant, in the train.

II. Mary Brooker

"Are you ill?"

"I am a little tired."

"You look as though you had seen a ghost. I am sure you are not well."

I did not feel well. I felt as though I had seen a ghost, and something worse than a ghost! I had found my way back to the hotel—how, I scarcely knew. The first person I met was Mrs. Jaynes. She was in the garden, which ran all round the building. My appearance seemed to occasion her anxiety.

"I am sure you are not well! Do sit down! Let me get you something to drink."

"Thanks; I will go to my own room. I have not been very well lately. A little upsets me."

She seemed reluctant to let me go. Her solicitude was flattering; though if there had been a little less of it I should have been equally content. She even offered me her arm. That I laughingly declined. I was not quite in such a piteous plight as to be in need of that. At last I escaped her. As I entered my sitting-room someone rose to greet me. It was Mr. Davis.

"Mr. Fountain, are you not well?"

My appearance seemed to strike him as it had struck the lady.

"I have had a shock. Will you ring the bell and order me some brandy?"

"A shock?" He looked at me curiously. "What sort of a shock?"

"I will tell you when you have ordered the brandy. I really am in need of something to revive me. I fancy my nervous system must be altogether out of order."

He rang the bell. I sank into an easy-chair, really grateful for the support which it afforded me. Although he sat still I was conscious that his eyes were on me all the time. When the waiter had brought the brandy Mr. Davis gave rein to his curiosity.

"I hope that nothing serious has happened."

"It depends upon what you call serious." I paused to allow the spirit to take effect. It did me good. "You remember what I told you about the strange sound which was uttered by the creature which robbed me in the train? I have heard that sound again."

"Indeed!" He observed me attentively. I had thought he would be sceptical; he was not. "Can you describe the sound?"

"It is difficult to describe, though when it is once heard it is impossible not to recognise it when it is heard again." I shuddered as I thought of it. "It is like the cry of some wild beast when in a state of frenzy—just a short, jerky, half-strangled yelp."

"May I ask what were the circumstances under which you heard it?"

"I was looking at the sea in front of Hesketh Crescent. I heard it close behind me, not once, but twice; and the second time I—I saw the face which I saw in the train."

I took another drink of brandy. I fancy that Mr. Davis saw how even the mere recollection affected me.

"Do you think that your assailant could by any possibility have been a woman?"

"A woman!"

"Was the face you saw anything like that?"

He produced from his pocket a pocket-book, and from the pocket-book a photograph. He handed it to me. I regarded it intently. It was not a good photograph, but it was a strange one. The more I looked at it the more it grew upon me that there was a likeness—a dim and fugitive likeness, but still a likeness, to the face which had glared at me only half an hour before.

"But surely this is not a woman?"

"Tell me, first of all, if you trace in it any resemblance."

"I do, and I don't. In the portrait the face, as I know it, is grossly flattered; and yet in the portrait it is sufficiently hideous."

Mr. Davis stood up. He seemed a little excited.

"I believe I have hit it!"

"You have hit it?"

"The portrait which you hold in your hand is the portrait of a criminal lunatic who escaped last week from Broadmoor."

"A criminal lunatic!"

As I looked at the portrait I perceived that it was the face of a lunatic.

"The woman—for it is a woman—is a perfect devil—as artful as she is wicked. She was there during Her Majesty's pleasure for a murder which was attended with details of horrible cruelty. She was more than suspected of having had a hand in other crimes. Since that portrait was taken she has deliberately burnt her face with a red-hot poker, disfiguring herself almost beyond recognition."

"There is another circumstance which I should mention, Mr. Davis. Do you know that this morning I saw the young gentle-man too?"

The detective stared.

"What young gentleman?"

"The young fellow who got into the train at Swindon, and who offered me his flask."

"You saw him! Where?"

"Here, in the hotel."

"The devil you did! And you spoke to him?"

"I tried to."

"And he hooked it?"

"That is the odd part of the thing. You will say there is something odd about everything I tell you; and I must confess there is. When you left me this morning I wrote a letter; when I had written it I left the room. As I was going along the corridor I saw, in front of me, the young man who was with me in the train."

"You are sure it was he?"

"Certain. When first I saw him he had his back to me. I suppose he heard me coming. Anyhow, he turned, and we were face to face. The recognition, I believe, was mutual, because as I advanced—"

"He cut his lucky?"

"He turned into a room upon his right."

"Of course you followed him?"

"I did. I made no bones about it. I was not three seconds after him, but when I entered, the room was empty."

"Empty!"

"It was an ordinary sitting-room like this, but on the other side of it there was a door. I tried that door. It was locked. I rapped with my knuckles. A woman answered."

"A woman?"

"A woman. She not only answered, she came out."

"Was she anything like that portrait?"

I laughed. The idea of instituting any comparison between the horror in the portrait and that vision of health and loveliness was too ludicrous.

"She was a lady who is stopping in the hotel, with whom I already had had some conversation, and who is about as unlike that portrait as anything could possibly be—a Mrs. Jaynes."

"Jaynes? A Mrs. Jaynes?" The detective bit his finger-nails. He seemed to be turning something over in his mind. "And did you see the man?"

"That is where the oddness of the thing comes in. She declared that there was no man."

"What do you mean?"

"She declared that no one had been near her bedroom while she had been in it. That there was no one in it at that particular moment is beyond a doubt, because she opened the door to let me see. I am inclined to think, upon reflection, that, after all, the man may have been concealed in the outer room, that I overlooked him in my haste, and that he made good his escape while I was knocking at the lady's door."

"But if he had a finger in the pie, that knocks the other theory upon the head." He nodded towards the portrait which I still was holding in my hand. "A man like that would scarcely have such a pal as Mary Brooker."

"I confess, Mr. Davis, that the whole affair is a mystery to me. I suppose that your theory is that the flask out of which I drank was drugged?"

"I should say upon the face of it that there can't be two doubts about that." The detective stood reflecting. "I should like to have a look at this Mrs. Jaynes. I will have a look at her. I'll go down to the office here, and I think it's just possible that I may be treated to a peep at her room."

When he had gone I was haunted by the thought of that criminal lunatic, who was at least so far sane that she had been able to make good her escape from Broadmoor. It was only when Mr. Davis had left me that I discovered that he had left the portrait behind him. I looked at it. What a face it was!

"Think," I said to myself, "of being left at the mercy of such a woman as that!"

The words had scarcely left my lips when, without any warning, the door of my room opened, and, just as I was taking it for granted that it was Mr. Davis come back for the portrait, in walked the young man with whom I had travelled in the train! He was dressed exactly as he had been yesterday, and wore the same indefinable but unmistakable something which denotes good breeding.

"Excuse me," he observed, as he stood with the handle of the door in one hand and his hat in the other, "but I believe you are the gentleman with whom I travelled yesterday from Swindon?" In my surprise I was for a moment tongue-tied. "I do not think I have made a mistake."

"No," I said, or rather stammered, "you have not made a mistake."

"It is only by a fortunate accident that I have just learnt that you are staying in the hotel. Pardon my intrusion, but when I changed carriages at Exeter I left behind me a cigar-case."

"A cigar-case?"

"Did you notice it? I thought it might have caught your eye. It was a present to me, and one I greatly valued. It matched this flask."

Coming a step or two towards me he held out a flask—the identical flask from which I had drunk! I stared alternately at him and at his flask.

"I was not aware that you changed carriages at Exeter."

"I wondered if you noticed it. I fancy you were asleep."

"A singular thing happened to me before I reached my journey's end—a singular and a disagreeable thing."

"How do you mean?"

"I was robbed."

"Robbed?"

"Did you notice anybody get into the carriage when you, as you say, got out?"

"Not that I am aware of. You know it was pretty dark. Why, good gracious! is it possible that after all it wasn't my imagination?"

"What wasn't your imagination?"

He came closer to me—so close that he touched my sleeve with his gloved hand.

"Do you know why I left the carriage when I did? I left it because I was bothered by the thought that there was someone in it besides us two."

"Someone in it besides us two?"

"Someone underneath the seat. I was dozing off as you were doing. More than once I woke up under the impression that someone was twitching my legs beneath the seat; pinching them—even pricking them."

"Did you not look to see if anyone was there?"

"You will laugh at me, but—I suppose I was silly—something restrained me. I preferred to make a bolt of it, and become the victim of my own imagination."

"You left me to become the victim of something besides your imagination, if what you say is correct."

All at once the stranger made a dart at the table. I suppose he had seen the portrait lying there, because, without any sort of ceremony, he picked it up and stared at it. As I observed him, commenting inwardly about the fellow's coolness, I distinctly saw a shudder pass all over him. Possibly it was a shudder of aversion, because, when he had stared his fill, he turned to me and asked—

"Who, may I ask, is this hideous-looking creature?"

"That is a criminal lunatic who has escaped from Broadmoor—one Mary Brooker."

"Mary Brooker! Mary Brooker! Mary Brooker's face will haunt me for many a day."

He laid the portrait down hesitatingly, as if it had for him some dreadful fascination which made him reluctant to let it go. Wholly at a loss what to say or do, whether to detain the man or to permit him to depart, I turned away and moved across the room. The instant I did so I heard behind me the sharp, frenzied yelp which I had heard in the train, and which I had heard again when I had been looking at the sea in front of Hesketh Crescent. I turned as on a pivot. The young man was staring at me.

"Did you hear that?" he said.

"Hear it! Of course I heard it."

"Good God!" He was shuddering so that it seemed to me that he could scarcely stand. "Do you know that it was that sound, coming from underneath the seat in the carriage, which made me make a bolt of it? I—I'm afraid you must excuse me. There there's my card. I'm staying at the 'Royal.' I will perhaps look you up again tomorrow."

Before I had recovered my presence of mind sufficiently to interfere he had moved to the door and was out of the room. As he went out Mr. Davis entered; they must have brushed each other as they passed.

"I forgot the portrait of that Brooker woman," Mr. Davis began.

"Why didn't you stop him?" I exclaimed.

"Stop whom?"

"Didn't you see him—the man who just went out?"

"Why should I stop him? Isn't he a friend of yours?"

"He's the man who travelled in the carriage with me from Swindon."

Davis was out of the room like a flash of lightning. When he returned he returned alone.

"Where is he?" I demanded.

"That's what I should like to know." Mr. Davis wiped his brow. "He must have travelled at the rate of about sixty miles an hour—he's nowhere to be seen. Whatever made you let him go?"

"He has left his card." I took it up. It was inscribed "George Etherege, Coliseum Club." "He says he is staying at the 'Royal Hotel.' I don't believe he had anything to do with the robbery. He came to me in the most natural manner possible to inquire for a cigar-case which he left behind him in the carriage. He says that while I was sleeping he changed carriages at Exeter because he suspected that someone was underneath the seat."

"Did he, indeed?"

"He says that he did not look to see if anybody was actually there because—well, something restrained him."

"I should like to have a little conversation with that young gentleman."

"I believe he speaks the truth, for this reason. While he was talking there came the sound which I have described to you before."

"The sort of bark?"

"The sort of bark. There was nothing to show from whence it came. I declare to you that it seemed to me that it came out of space. I never saw a man so frightened as he was. As he stood trembling, just where you are standing now, he stammered out that it was because he had heard that sound come from underneath the seat in the carriage that he had decided that discretion was the better part of valour, and, instead of gratifying his curiosity, had chosen to retreat."

III. The Secret of the Mask

Table d'hôte had commenced when I sat down. My right-hand neighbour was Mrs. Jaynes. She asked me if I still suffered any ill effects from my fatigue.

"I suppose," she said, when I assured her that all ill effects had passed away, "that you have not thought anything of what I said to you this morning—about my theory of the mask?"

I confessed that I had not.

"You should. It is a subject which is a crotchet of mine, and to which I have devoted many years—many curious years of my life."

"I own that, personally, I do not see exactly where the interest comes in."

"No? Do me a favour. Come to my sitting-room after dinner, and I will show you where the interest comes in."

"How do you mean?"

"Come and see."

She amused me. I went and saw. Dinner being finished, her proceedings, when together we entered her apartment—that apartment which in the morning I thought I had seen entered by my fellow-passenger—took me a little by surprise.

"Now I am going to make you my confidant—you, an entire stranger—you, whom I never saw in my life before this morning. I am a judge of character, and in you I feel that I may place implicit confidence. I am going to show you all my secrets; I am going to induct you into the hidden mysteries; I am going to lay bare before you the mind of an inventor. But it doesn't follow because I have confidence in you that I have confidence in all the world besides, so, before we begin, if you please, I will lock the door."

As she was suiting the action to the word I ventured to remonstrate.

"But, my dear madam, don't you think—"

"I think nothing. I know that I don't wish to be taken unawares, and to have published what I have devoted the better portion of my life to keeping secret."

"But if these matters are of such a confidential nature I assure you—"

"My good sir, I lock the door."

She did. I was sorry that I had accepted so hastily her invitation, but I yielded. The door was locked. Going to the fireplace she leaned her arm upon the mantel-shelf.

"Did it ever occur to you," she asked, "what possibilities might be open to us if, for instance, Smith could temporarily become Jones?"

"I don't quite follow you," I said. I did not.

"Suppose that you could at will become another person, and in the character of that other person could move about unrecognised among your friends, what lessons you might learn!"

"I suspect," I murmured, "that they would for the most part be lessons of a decidedly unpleasant kind."

"Carry the idea a step further. Think of the possibilities of a dual existence. Think of living two distinct and separate lives. Think of doing as Robinson what you condemn as Brown. Think of doubling the parts and hiding within your own breast the secret of the double; think of leading a triple life; think of leading many lives in one—of being the old man and the young, the husband and the wife, the father and the son."

"Think, in other words, of the unattainable."

"Not unattainable!" Moving away from the mantel-shelf she raised her hand above her head with a gesture which was all at once dramatic. "I have attained!"

"You have attained? To what?"

"To the multiple existence. It is the secret of the mask. I told myself some years ago that it ought to be possible to make a mask which should in every respect so closely resemble the human countenance that it would be difficult, if not impossible, even under the most trying conditions, to tell the false face from the real. I made experiments. I succeeded. I learnt the secret of the mask. Look at that."

She took a leather case from her pocket. Abstracting its contents, she handed them to me. I was holding in my hand what seemed to me to be a preparation of some sort of skin—gold-beater's skin, it might have been. On one side it was curiously, and even delicately, painted. On the other side there were fastened to the skin some oddly-shaped bosses or pads. The whole affair, I suppose, did not weigh half an ounce. While I was examining it Mrs. Jaynes stood looking down at me.

"You hold in your hand," she said, "the secret of the mask. Give it to me."

I gave it to her. With it in her hand she disappeared into the room beyond. Hardly had she vanished than the bedroom door reopened, and an old lady came out.

"My daughter begs you will excuse her." She was a quaint old lady, about sixty years of age, with silver hair, and the corkscrew ringlets of a bygone day. "My daughter is not very ceremonious, and is so wrapt up in what she calls her experiments that I sometimes tell her she is wanting in consideration. While she is making her preparations, perhaps you will allow me to offer you a cup of tea."

The old lady carried a canister in her hand, which, apparently, contained tea. A tea-service was standing on a little side-table; a kettle was singing on the hob. The old lady began to measure out the tea into the teapot.

"We always carry our tea with us. Neither my daughter nor I care for the tea which they give you in hotels."

I meekly acquiesced. To tell the truth, I was a trifle bewildered. I had had no idea that Mrs. Jaynes was accompanied by her mother. Had not the old lady come out of the room immediately after the young one had gone into it I should have suspected a trick—that I was being made the subject of experiment with the mysterious "mask."

As it was, I was more than half inclined to ask her if she was really what she seemed to be. But I decided—as it turned out most unfortunately—to keep my own counsel and to watch the sequence of events. Pouring me out a cup of tea, the old lady seated herself on a low chair in front of the fire.

"My daughter thinks a great deal of her experiments. I hope you will not encourage her. She quite frightens me at times; she says such dreadful things."

I sipped my tea and smiled.

"I don't think there is much cause for fear."

"No cause for fear when she tells one that she might commit a murder; that a hundred thousand people might see her do it, and that not by any possibility could the crime be brought home to her!"

"Perhaps she exaggerates a little."

"Do you think that she can hear?"

The old lady glanced round in the direction of the bedroom door.

"You should know better than I. Perhaps it would be as well to say nothing which you would not like her to hear."

"But I must tell someone. It frightens me. She says it is a dream she had."

"I don't think, if I were you, I would pay much attention to a dream."

The old lady rose from her seat. I did not altogether like her manner. She came and stood in front of me, rubbing her hands, nervously, one over the other. She certainly seemed considerably disturbed.

"She came down yesterday from London, and she says she dreamed that she tried one of her experiments—in the train."

"In the train!"

"And in order that her experiment might be thorough she robbed a man."

"She robbed a man!"

"And in her pocket I found this."

The old lady held out my watch and chain! It was unmistakable. The watch was a hunter. I could see that my crest and monogram were engraved upon the case. I stood up. The strangest part of the affair was that when I gained my feet it seemed as though something had happened to my legs—I could not move them. Probably something in my demeanour struck the old lady as strange. She smiled at me.

"What is the matter with you? Why do you look so funny?" she exclaimed.

"That is my watch and chain."

"Your watch and chain—yours! Then why don't you take them?"

She held them out to me in her extended palm. She was not six feet from where I stood, yet I could not reach them. My feet seemed glued to the floor.

"I—I cannot move. Something has happened to my legs."

"Perhaps it is the tea. I will go and tell my daughter."

Before I could say a word to stop her she was gone. I was fastened like a post to the ground. What had happened to me was more than I could say. It had all come in an instant. I felt as I had felt in the railway carriage the day before—as though I were in a dream. I looked around me. I saw the teacup on the little table at my side, I saw the flickering fire, I saw the shaded lamps; I was conscious of the presence of all these things, but I saw them as if I saw them in a dream. A sense of nausea was stealing over me—a sense of horror. I was afraid of I knew not what. I was unable to ward off or to control my fear.

I cannot say how long I stood there—certainly some minutes—helpless, struggling against the pressure which seemed to weigh upon my brain. Suddenly, without any sort of warning, the bedroom door opened, and there walked into the room the young man who, before dinner, had visited me in my own apartment, and who yesterday had travelled with me in the train. He came straight across the room, and, with the most perfect coolness, stood right in front of me. I could see that in his shirt-front were my studs. When he raised his hands I could see that in his wristbands were my links. I could see that he was wearing my watch and chain. He was actually holding my watch in his hand when he addressed me.

"I have only half a minute to spare, but I wanted to speak to you about—Mary Brooker. I saw her portrait in your room—you remember? She's what is called a criminal lunatic, and she's escaped from Broadmoor. Let me see, I think it was a week today, and just about this time—no, it's now a quarter to nine; it was just after nine." He slipped my watch into his waistcoat-pocket. "She's still at large, you know. They're on the look-out for her all over England, but she's still at large. They say she's a lunatic. There are lunatics at Broadmoor, but she's not one. She's no more a lunatic than you or I."

He touched me lightly on the chest; such was my extreme disgust at being brought into physical contact with him that even before the slight pressure of his fingers my legs gave way under me, and I sank back into my chair.

"You're not asleep?"

"No," I said, "I'm not asleep."

Even in my stupefied condition I was conscious of a desire to leap up and take him by the throat. Nothing of this, however, was portrayed upon my face, or, at any rate, he showed no sign of being struck by it.

"She's a misunderstood genius, that's what Mary Brooker is. She has her tastes and people do not understand them; she likes to kill—to kill! One of these days she means to kill herself, but in the meantime she takes pleasure in killing others."

Seating himself on a corner of the table at my side, allowing one foot to rest upon the ground, he swung the other in the air.

"She's a bit of an actress too. She wanted to go upon the stage, but they said that she was mad. They were jealous, that's what it was. She's the finest actress in the world. Her acting would deceive the devil himself—they allowed that even at Broadmoor—but she only uses her powers for acting to gratify her taste—for killing. It was only the other day she bought this knife."

He took, apparently out of the bosom of his vest, a long, glittering, cruel-looking knife.

"It's sharp. Feel the point—and the edge."

He held it out towards me. I did not attempt to touch it; it is probable that I should not have succeeded even if I had attempted.

"You won't? Well, perhaps you're right. It's not much fun killing people with a knife. A knife's all very well for cutting them up afterwards, but she likes to do the actual killing with her own hands and nails. I shouldn't be surprised if, one of these days, she were to kill you—perhaps to-night. It is a long time since she killed anyone, and she is hungry. Sorry I can't stay; but this day week she escaped from Broadmoor as the clock had finished striking nine, and it only wants ten minutes, you see."

He looked at my watch, even holding it out for me to see.

"Good-night."

With a careless nod he moved across the room, holding the glittering knife in his hand. When he reached the bedroom door he turned and smiled, Raising the knife he waved it towards me in the air; then he disappeared into the inner room.

I was again alone—possibly for a minute or more; but this time it seemed to me that my solitude continued only for a few fleeting seconds. Perhaps the time went faster because I felt, or thought I felt, that the pressure on my brain was giving way, that I only had to make an effort of sufficient force to be myself again and free. The power of making such an effort was temporarily absent, but something within seemed to tell me that at any moment it might return. The bedroom door—that door which, even as I look back, seems to have been really and truly a door in some unpleasant dream—reopened. Mrs. Jaynes came in; with rapid strides she swept across the room; she had something in her right hand, which she threw upon the table.

"Well," she cried, "what do you think of the secret of the mask?"

"The secret of the mask?"

Although my limbs were powerless throughout it all I retained, to a certain extent, the control of my own voice.

"See here, it is such a little thing." She picked up the two objects which she had thrown upon the table. One of them was the preparation of some sort of skin which she had shown to me before. "These are the masks. You would not think that they were perfect representations of the human face—that masterpiece of creative art—and yet they are. All the world would be deceived by them as you have been. This is an old woman's face, this is the face of a young man." As she held them up I could see, though still a little dimly, that the objects which she dangled before my eyes were, as she said, veritable masks. "So perfect are they, they might have been skinned from the fronts of living creatures. They are such little things, yet I have made them with what toil! They have been the work of years, these two, and just one other. You see nothing satisfied me but perfection; I have made hundreds to make these two. People could not make out what I was doing; they thought that I was making toys; I told them that I was. They smiled at me; they thought that it was a new phase of madness. If that be so, then in madness there is more cool, enduring, unconquerable resolution than in all your sanity. I meant to conquer, and I did. Failure did not dishearten me; I went straight on. I had a purpose to fulfil; I would have fulfilled it even though I should have had first to die. Well, it is fulfilled."

Turning, she flung the masks into the fire; they were immediately in flames. She pointed to them as they burned.

"The labour of years is soon consumed. But I should not have triumphed had I not been endowed with genius—the genius of the actor's art. I told myself that I would play certain parts—parts which would fit the masks—and that I would be the parts I played. Not only across the footlights, not only with a certain amount of space between my audience and me, not only for the passing hour, but, if I chose, for ever and for aye. So all through the years I rehearsed these parts when I was not engaged upon the masks. That, they thought, was madness in another phase. One of the parts"—she came closer to me; her voice became shriller—"one of the parts was that of an old woman. Have you seen her? She is in the fire." She jerked her thumb in the direction of the fireplace. "Her part is played—she had to see that the tea was drunk. Another of the parts was that of a young gentleman. Think of my playing the man! Absurd. For there is that about a woman which is not to be disguised. She always reveals her sex when she puts on men's clothes. You noticed it, did you not—when, before dinner, he came to you; when you saw him in the corridor this morning; when yesterday he spent an hour with you in the train? I know you noticed it because of these."

She drew out of her pocket a handful of things. There were my links, my studs, my watch and chain, and other properties of mine. Although the influence of the drug which had been administered to me in the tea was passing off, I felt, even more than ever, as though I were an actor in a dream.

"The third part which I chose to play was the part of—Mrs. Jaynes!"

Clasping her hands behind her back, she posed in front of me in an attitude which was essentially dramatic.

"Look at me well. Scan all my points. Appraise me. You say that I am beautiful. I saw that you admired my hair, which flows loose upon my shoulders"—she unloosed the fastenings of her hair so that it did flow loose upon her shoulders—"the bloom upon my cheeks, the dimple in my chin, my face in its entirety. It is the secret of the mask, my friend, the secret of the mask! You ask me why I have watched, and toiled, and schemed to make the secret mine."

She stretched out her hand with an uncanny gesture. "Because I wished to gratify my taste for killing. Yesterday I might have killed you; to-night I will."

She did something to her head and dress. There was a rustle of drapery. It was like a conjurer's change. Mrs. Jaynes had gone, and instead there stood before me the creature with, as I had described it to Davis, the face of a devil—the face I had seen in the train. The transformation in its entirety was wonderful. Mrs. Jaynes was a fine, stately woman with a swelling bust and in the prime of life. This was a lank, scraggy creature, with short, grey hair—fifty if a day. The change extended even to the voice. Mrs. Jaynes had the soft, cultivated accents of a lady. This creature shrieked rather than spoke.

"I," she screamed, "am Mary Brooker. It is a week today since I won freedom. The bloodhounds are everywhere upon my track. They are drawing near. But they shall not have me till I have first of all had you."

She came closer, crouching forward, glaring at me with a maniac's eyes. From her lips there came that hideous cry, half gasp, half yelp, which had haunted me since the day before, when I heard it in my stupor in the train.

"I scratched you yesterday. I bit you. I sucked your blood. Now I will suck it dry, for you are mine."

She reckoned without her host. I had only sipped the tea. I had not, as I had doubtless been intended to do, emptied the cup. I was again master of myself; I was only awaiting a favourable opportunity to close. I meant to fight for life.

She came nearer to me and nearer, uttering all the time that blood-curdling sound which was so like the frenzied cry of some maddened animal. When her extended hands were all but touching me I rose up and took her by the throat. She had evidently supposed that I was still under the influence of the drug, because when I seized her she gave a shriek of astonished rage. I had taken her unawares. I had her over on her back. But I soon found that I had undertaken more than I could carry through. She had not only the face of a devil, she had the strength of one. She flung me off as easily as though I were a child. In her turn she had me down upon my back. Her fingers closed about my neck. I could not shake her off. She was strangling me.

She would have strangled me—she nearly did. When, attracted by the creature's hideous cries, which were heard from without, they forced their way into the room, they found me lying unconscious, and, as they thought, dead, upon the floor. For days I hung between life and death. When life did come back again Mary Brooker was once more an inmate of Her Majesty's house of detention at Broadmoor.

An Experience

I. Before Dinner

"I was walking along the shore towards Goring. It was pitch dark. The tide was out. I could see the wet sands gleaming in the darkness. Far out at sea were the lights of two fishing-boats. And that was all. On the landward side there was not a glimmer. The place was a howling wilderness. It was just as though I were alone in space. A keen north-west breeze was blowing. I could hear the moan of the receding waves. The sound seemed to come from miles away. It was cold."

The speaker paused. He seemed to be describing, when he continued, a scene which was actually at that moment taking place before his eyes.

"I suppose that my thoughts, like the scene, were sombre. Perhaps a touch of the eeriness of my surroundings had got into my veins. It may have done. I believe it had. For as I walked along I began to be haunted by a curious fancy—the fancy that I was not alone. It was absurd. There was not a sound. There was no one else in sight. But there it was the feeling that someone else was close at hand. I told myself it was absurd. I even stopped, and as I peered about me in the gloom I called myself hard names. But when I again went on with me there went the fancy too. And—"

Again the speaker paused. We were in the public room of the hotel. At that hour, with the exception of him and me, the great room was deserted. We were seated at a little table which was before a window. The twilight was gathering. The gas was not yet lighted. The room was in shadow. As he leaned forward and laid his hand lightly on my wrist I was conscious of a feeling which positively amounted to a shudder. As he himself had said, the thing was absurd; but there it was.

"And I had not gone fifty yards, when I heard a footstep at my side."

The statement contained nothing which could in itself be called in any way remarkable, but, to use a commonplace, as he uttered it I felt my blood turn cold.

"Just one footstep—the sound of a foot falling softly on the pebbly ground. It was close to my side, on my right. I turned and looked. There was no one there. I told myself I was deluded, that my imagination, preternaturally alert, was playing me a trick. I went on. I had not gone a dozen feet when the footstep came again. I said to myself—

"'You are a fool, my friend. Your brain is over-excited. You are just in that state of mind in which fancy plays one tricks.'

"But the footstep came again. This time there were two of them—the sound of two feet falling rhythmically, just for all the world as though someone were walking at my side and keeping pace with me. I walked on, seeming to pay no heed. I asked myself if by any chance the thing could be an echo. As I was endeavouring to turn the matter over in my mind someone touched me on my right arm.

"I started—I don't mind owning to you I started. With an exclamation I turned round. There was no one there."

The speaker withdrew his hand from my wrist. He raised it to his brow.

"I confess that when I perceived that there was no one there I was amazed. The touch had been so real. And yet, after all, perhaps my imagination was again to blame. I went on. I walked perhaps another dozen yards. Then it came again—the touch! Although I was half expecting it, I wheeled round in a sort of rage, and saw a face staring at me in the darkness.

"My friend—although you are a stranger, sir, to me, I trust you will forgive me if I say my friend—I am free to own that I felt as though my heart had ceased to beat. The face was quite distinct, although I could not make up my mind if it was the face of a man or a devil. As I looked at it it vanished."

The stranger drew a long breath. He paused again. For my own part I see no reason to conceal the fact that I was glad he did. He had such a horrible way of telling what I saw bade fair to be a "horrible tale," that I should have been glad if he had paused for good. Although, for some cause, I felt incapable of putting this desire of mine into words, it was not lessened by a suspicion which was dawning on me that the stranger was scarcely in his sober senses. He seemed to read my thoughts.

"You think that I was mad. Or, at least, that I was in one of those conditions of mind and of body in which hallucinations crowd upon the mind. For the moment I thought so too. I walked on at an increased pace, determined to throw off the curious sense of depression which seemed to weigh me down. The place was solitary. The air was fresh; the breeze was keen. It would be easy to relieve the fever which I supposed was in my brain; but my expectation was not realised. The steps went with me, the touch was on my arm, the face came back again. It was impossible this time to doubt that it was a face, for I saw now that it was attached to a body, and that the body was that of a man. He was quite close to me, within twelve inches, and he held my arm firmly in his grip. There was no mistake about that grip, for there are the finger marks still upon my skin. But where he had come from, out of the darkness, was more than I could understand.

"We looked at each other, as I judge, for seconds, then I found my voice.

"'Who are you?'

"He laughed. My friend"—again the stranger, leaning across the little table, laid his hand upon my wrist. I wished he wouldn't—"it is so easy to speak of certain things, it is so hard to bring them home to a listener's mind. That man's laughter froze the marrow in my bones. As he laughed he vanished into space. I could hear his laughter even after he himself had gone; and though I could see nothing there, and no one, I still felt his touch upon my arm, and could hear him laughing at my side.

"It was some seconds before I realised the fact that he had disappeared—it was hard to realise it while I yet was conscious of that iron grip. But at last I tore myself away, and, performing a right-about face, I returned towards the Worthing lights."

The stranger indulged in another of his ominous pauses. Taking out his handkerchief, he wiped his ringers and the palms of his hands. My situation reminded me of the wedding guest "fixed" by the ancient mariner. I hoped his tale was nearly done. There was an uncanniness about his tone which I am unable to describe.

"But, as I went, the steps went with me. The touch continually returned upon my arm. I quickened. The steps were quickened too. I slowed. The steps were slowed. I broke into a run. The steps ran with me. They were sometimes in front, and sometimes behind; sometimes on my left, and sometimes on my right; sometimes, as I live and breathe, above me in the air. And the laughter came and went. And the man, my friend, the man came and vanished—vanished and came. The man! The man!"

Placing his elbows on the table, the stranger hid his face within his hands. Even in the twilight I could see him shudder. Had I followed my natural impulse I should have risen to my feet and sneaked from the room. But I felt that he might catch me in the act. While I hesitated, feeling that I could have said a good deal—only I couldn't—the stranger removed his hands. His face looked ghastly white.

"That was three nights ago. Time enough, you say, to have forgotten my illusions. My friend"—I wished most heartily that he would not persist in calling me his friend—"that man, his laugh, and his steps have been with me at intervals ever since. In the darkness and in the light, in public and in private, in the street and in my room. I am listening and watching all the time. My friend, do you not hear his laughter? Listen! There are footsteps on the stairs!"

Again the stranger, leaning over the table, caught me by the wrist.

I may mention, in order that you may thoroughly understand how entire had been the absence of enjoyment with which I had listened to the stranger's pleasing little anecdote, that I have a constitutional objection to stories of the supernatural. As a child, merely to come across the words "ghost story" was to fill me with a sense of sickening repulsion. There was a time in my life when if a person had insisted on pouring into my unwilling ears a tale of "spooks," that person would have enjoyed the idiomatic pleasure of seeing me "driven into fits." Even now on such subjects I am of an extremely nervous temperament, and by the time the stranger had got so far I was not sure, of my own knowledge, if I was standing on my head or heels. When he grasped my wrist I felt as I may safely say I never felt before. I was speechless.

"Listen! Those are his footsteps coming up the stairs. One, two! One, two! Can you not hear them coming, step by step?"

I distinctly could hear something, and the feelings with which I heard it are altogether indescribable. Suddenly the stranger's manner changed. He loosed my wrist.

He rose to his feet. Almost unconsciously I rose with him.

"Listen! He is gone! Ha! Someone else is coming. But it is not he."

It was not "he," unless "he" was the waiter. That functionary had come to light the gas. He seemed startled when he saw us standing there—and well he might have been. To see two men standing facing each other across a narrow table, with faces as white as sheets, trembling like leaves—I know that I could feel my knees going pit-a-pat one against the other—was a sight calculated to cause a surprise even in a waiter's breast. But he held his peace. He lit the gas. He drew the blinds. He went away.

When he had gone, the stranger, turning, fixed his glance again on me. As he did so I was conscious that his glance had on me a very curious effect. I felt that I could not escape it. It held me with a species of fascination. As I had never seen the man in my life before, he was in the most literal sense of the word a stranger. I had been sitting in solitary state, in the half-light of the autumnal afternoon, looking out upon the sea. He had come in and found me there. Coming to the table at which I sat, he had entered into conversation—conversation which had drifted into that exhilarating little story of his stroll towards Goring. In the imperfect light I had not been able to make out what manner of man he was. Now I saw—though, I own, still dimly—that he was tall—unusually tall, with striking, clean-shaven face, and a remarkable pair of eyes. His manner, too, was singularly impressive—I protest that I found it so, at any rate. Raising his arm, he pointed at me with the index finger of his right hand.

"You see, it is light, but I still watch and listen. I know that he will come. Did I not say so? Hark! Do you not hear the steps coming up the stairs? It is the man!"

As before, I heard the sound of footsteps coming up the stairs. Supremely silly though it was—and, worst of all, I knew that it was silly—the sound made me feel sick.

"See! The door is opening."

I turned. The door was opening, apparently of its own accord, for it stood wide open, and there was no one there. I stood staring like a fool for some seconds, I imagine, when the stranger, leaning forward, almost whispered in my ear—

"It is the man!"

It was a man, for at that instant a man came in. He was a great ungainly-looking fellow. He appeared to me to be deformed. He had the ugliest head and face I ever saw upon a pair of shoulders. He slouched rather than walked. He wore no cap, and his hair was in the wildest disarray. His dress—he wore a sort of nondescript fisherman's costume—was anything but suited to the place in which he was. He stood just within the door, staring at me with half-sullen, half-ferocious eyes. With an effort which surprised myself, I drew myself together.

"Don't talk nonsense!" I cried. "There is nothing strange about the man. He is only a fisherman. He has doubtless business with someone here in the hotel."

The stranger only said—

"He comes this way."

He did, moving towards us across the room with an awkward method of progression, which curiously recalled the movements of a crab. He advanced to within three feet of where we were. Had I chosen I might have reached out and touched him with my hand.

"He is gone!"

It seems absurd to write it, but he was, and from before our eyes.

"The door has closed!"

It had, with a sullen bang. Where the man had gone to or who had closed the door were problems which at the moment I did not attempt to solve. The stranger drew himself up straight. There was a ring of triumph in his tone.

"Was it a delusion? Am I mad?"

A minute before I should have been prepared to say he was. Then I was more than half inclined to think that we, both of us, were mad together. As I was trying to collect my scattered senses—they were very scattered senses, too!—the stranger whirled round with a vigour and suddenness which were anything but soothing.

"He has you by the arm!"

As he spoke, a grip fastened on my arm which compressed the limb as if it were being held within an iron vice. I turned, half in terror, half in pain. The man was standing on my left, grasping me with his hideous paw, though how he had got there, unless he came through the solid wall, is more than I can say. I struck out at him in a spasm of sudden rage; but, before the blow could reach him, he was gone.

"You heard his laughter!"

Did I? Didn't I! It was ringing in my ears, although the man himself had fled—an unearthly peal, such as we might fancy coming from a fiend in hell.

"Ring the bell," I gasped. "For God's sake ring the bell!"

"What good can that do? That will not keep him from us. He comes to me when I am in the crowded street. Ssh! He is here!"

He was; this time upon my right. He stood at a distance of some five or six feet, eyeing me with a savage leer. I gazed at him transfixed. He seemed to take a malignant pleasure in my evident distress. After a momentary pause he put his hand into his blouse, and drew from it a knife. It was a long, thin knife such as butchers use. He looked alternately at the knife and at me. Then, holding it in his left hand, he began to smooth it upon the palm of his right.

"I wonder," whispered the stranger, "if it is for your throat or mine."

I really didn't know—I won't say I didn't care, but I certainly had no disposition to inquire. The man continued to draw the knife backwards and forwards on the palm of his hand, fixing on me, all the time, a glance of peculiar malignancy.

"Put up that knife!" I said.

"Knife!" he answered, in a sort of echo.

"Do you hear? Put away that knife!"

"Knife!" he echoed.

I advanced towards him with a degree of decision which filled me with amazement.

"You think you can frighten us. You play your tricks very well, but take my advice and don't go too far. Put up that knife or give it to me!"

His only answer was to raise the weapon threateningly in the air.

"Take care!" cried the stranger; "he will stab you."

"We shall see."

I sprang at him; we grappled. He struggled fiercely in my arms, then he collapsed as if he were a bladder—there was nothing there. But, at my feet, his knife was lying on the ground.

"He has left his knife," said the stranger. I saw that plainly; it was the only thing there was to see. "Pick it up."

I picked it up. I examined it as I held it in my hand. The thing was real enough, but where had its owner gone? I carried it to the table. I laid it down. I took out my handkerchief and wiped my brow. I was conscious that the stranger's eyes were on me all the time. I was conscious, too, that my brain was in a whirl. I felt as if all these things were happening in a dream; that they were but fictions; that I was in a nightmare from which, if I could but make an effort, I should awake. It seemed to me that some function of the brain had ceased to do its work, that something had snapped. Was I mad? I had read somewhere that the state of madness was rendered worse by the fact that madmen were themselves aware, though perhaps but vaguely, of their condition. Was it possible that I, without a moment's warning, had crossed the border-line which divides the sane man from the mad? Were we, then, a pair of lunatics?

The knife was real enough, there was no question about that. I eyed it keenly as it lay upon the table, as ugly a looking weapon as one would care to see. I put out my hand to take it up. I already had it by the handle, when it was snatched away. Again that appalling laughter rang in my ears. Looking up, there was the owner back again.

When I perceived that this was the case I endeavoured, so to speak, to steady my mind. Was the thing an optical delusion? Was I the victim of hallucination? Such an explanation seemed opposed to common sense, yet I had sense enough to know that the facts, as they appeared, were more in opposition still.

I turned to the stranger.

"Are you sure that there is someone there?"

He shrugged his shoulders.

"Are not you?"

"Frankly, I am not. But I should like to be."

"Suppose you go and take him by the hand."

"I will."

The man had resumed his previous occupation of drawing the flat side of the knife backwards and forwards upon his open palm. I advanced towards him with outstretched hand.

"Will you not shake hands?"

He immediately grasped my hand in his, and, advancing his knife, drew the sharp edge across the back of my knuckles. As he did so he laughed. I snatched my hand away. He had cut the skin so that the blood flowed freely. It was an act of wanton savagery.

"You cur!"

I applied my handkerchief to staunch the flow of blood. Immediately the white linen showed a vivid stain. As I was reflecting on this unpleasant proof of the man's corporality—and of the corporality of his knife—the door opened, and my wife came in. My first impulse, when I saw her enter, was to get her out again. The idea of her remaining, even for a second, in the same room with such a ruffian was unendurable. I hurried to her.

"Ada, come away!"

I was about to take her by the hand and lead her from the room. But she, drawing back a little, looked at me with apparent surprise.

"Why? What do you want? The dinner-bell will ring in a minute."

"Never mind the dinner-bell. We will wait for that below. I do not wish you to remain with that man."

"Man? What man? Do you mean the gentleman who is standing at the table?"

Turning, I saw that she was looking at the stranger. But between him and us was the fellow with the knife. He was still smoothing the blade upon his palm, and still glaring at me with his malignant leer.

I dropped my voice. "Not that one; the other."

"The other? What do you mean?"

Stretching out my hand, I removed my handkerchief so that she could see the wound, from which the blood still trickled.

"Look what he has done with that knife of his. The fellow is unsafe. Come with me. I mean to send for the police."

I could not tell if it was my words, or the sight of my wound, or the sight of the man, which caused her to shrink away from me. A startled look was on her face.

"Raymond, what are you talking about? There is no one here except this gentleman and you."

The stranger interposed.

"There has been someone here. But he has gone. Now we are alone."

I looked. It was as he said—the man had gone. But, as before, where or how was more than I could say. I knew enough of his peculiarities to be aware that the fact of his having gone was no guarantee that he would not immediately return.

II. At Dinner

While I was hesitating what to do, my wife, moving to the stranger, broke into an animated conversation. It seemed to me that her manner was a trifle forced. Her words came to me as though I heard them in a dream.

"Beautiful weather, hasn't it been? Quite lovely. I have had such a delicious walk along the shore towards Goring."

"It is a charming walk towards Goring—especially at night."

I have never been that way at night. I should think it's rather lonely, isn't it? Raymond, what are you standing there for? You look as though you were moonstruck. Come here, do."

"I—I was thinking."

"Very civil of you. Come here."

I went to her. She was on my left, the stranger on my right. All at once he whispered in my ear—

"He has come back again."

I whirled right round. He had—the man. He was at that moment coming through the door. Moving rapidly across the room, he came straight to me. He held out to me his knife.

"Confound you!" I exclaimed.

I clenched my fist to strike at him. The stranger tapped me on the shoulder. "He has gone!"

He had—in front of me was Charlie Oates. Oates laughed.

"What's the matter? You look ferocious. Do you want to murder me?"

"Gates! You!"

"Of course it's me! Didn't you know me? I thought that I was recognisable."

"Of course, I know you. Only I didn't see you coming. You took me by surprise."

I glanced uneasily about the room. Where had that scoundrel gone? My wife laid her hand upon my arm. From her tone I perceived she was uneasy.

"Raymond, are you unwell?"

"I am quite well. Only this sort of thing is rather startling."

"What sort of thing?"

"Don't you call it startling when a man comes and goes in this eccentric manner?"

My wife was silent. Looking at her, I saw that her eyes were open at their widest.

"Are you alluding to me?" asked Oates with a laugh. "I wasn't aware that my comings and goings could be called eccentric."

"Of course I wasn't. But there's the dinner-bell! I'll just run upstairs and attend to my hand."

"What is the matter with your hand?" asked Ada.

"Can't you see?"

I held it out in front of me. The stranger spoke.

"There is nothing the matter with your hand."

There wasn't—or, at least, there didn't seem to be.

"Well," I cried, "this is the very latest! Talk about the quickest thing in cures! And—why, there isn't even a stain upon my handkerchief! What's become of all the blood?" I turned to the stranger. "You saw him draw his knife across my knuckles."

My wife struck in—

"Saw who draw his knife across your knuckles? Raymond, what are you talking about?" She addressed the stranger. "What is he talking about?"

The stranger bowed.

"You should know better than I!"

As he bowed I distinctly saw him wink at me. I presumed that he intended to convey a hint that it would be just as well to keep our little adventure to ourselves. I took what I believe in sporting circles is called "the tip."

"Come along, Ada; they will have begun dinner before we get there."

Unceremoniously I slipped her arm through mine. Before this several other persons had put in an appearance. They, with one accord, were moving towards the dining-room. Among them were Oates and the stranger. But the wife hung back.

"Raymond, do you think you had better go down to dinner?"

"My good child, what do you mean? I'm starving!"

"But are you sure you are quite well?"

"I'm well enough; but—" I glanced after the stranger. His back was turned to me. He was going through the doorway, with Oates at his side. "The fact is, I have had an adventure. It has a little upset me."

"What sort of an adventure?"

"Rather a curious one. I will tell you about it afterwards."

"Why not tell me about it now, Raymond? You make me feel concerned; you seem so strange."

I was hesitating whether I should or should not tell her there and then, when a voice said, speaking, as it appeared, quite close to my ear—

"Come down to dinner!"

I turned with a start.

"By Jove!" I cried. "Who was that?"

"Who was what? I heard nothing. There is no one here. Raymond, what is wrong?"

"There is nothing wrong. Only I—I suppose I'm hungry. Don't let's stop here, my dear; let's get downstairs."

I did not wait for her reply; I gave her no chance to make one. I am afraid I almost dragged her from the room. Catching her arm tightly in mine, I moved quickly towards the door before she had an opportunity to speak. I fancy that my method of proceeding took her breath away. I hurried with her down the stairs, and into the dining-room, in a style which must have led anyone who watched our progress to suppose that we were afraid that, if we did not make haste, all the dinner would be gone. I placed her in a seat.

"Raymond," she demanded, as I took the chair beside her, "are you mad?"

"That, my dear, is a question which I have seriously asked myself already."

She looked at me with an expression in her eyes of absolute terror. I pretended not to notice it. They were serving the soup. While they did so, I looked up and down the table. In front of me was the stranger. Something caused me to be aware of it, although I did not see him. I made quite an effort to prevent my eyes travelling in his direction. I ate my soup without once glancing up from my plate. At the same time I was conscious that my wife was not eating hers; I felt that she was watching me. While they were handing round the fish I did glance up. My eyes rested for a moment on the stranger sitting opposite. As they did so he said in a low tone, which yet was distinctly audible to me, "He is here again!"

"Where?"

"Leaning over your shoulder!"

I turned with a shudder of irresistible repugnance. I nearly dashed my head against the scoundrel's face. He was actually leaning over my shoulder, peering into my face with his hideous leer. I rose from my chair.

"You villain!" I exclaimed.

Although my back was turned to the stranger, I heard him say behind me, "He is gone!"

He was—like a flash of lightning. I sank back into my chair with a feeling of inconceivable amazement.

"Raymond, what are you doing?"

My wife, as she put the question, seemed to be in a state of nervous agitation.

"Nothing. I—I fancy I must have a touch of indigestion."

I perceived that the tears were standing in her eyes.

"I am sure you are not well."

"Don't make a scene, my dear; I am quite well. Only—only this sort of thing is startling."

"I should think it was." This I heard the young fellow who was sitting next to me mutter to his friend. "I should say he had got 'em again."

He appeared to be under the extraordinary impression that I was suffering from the effects of dipsomania, which was agreeable hearing to a man who had all his life been a total abstainer from strong drink. But, saying nothing, and endeavouring to steady my nerves—my hands were trembling—I attacked my fish.

"Don't you hear him laughing?"

I had scarcely swallowed a mouthful when the stranger put this question to me from across the table. The moment he had put it a peal of horrible laughter rang through the room. I laid down my knife and fork.

"The villain ought not to be allowed in the room. Where is the man?"

The young fellow who had made that uncomplimentary remark about my having "got 'em again" seemed to think that the question was addressed to him.

"What man?" he asked.

"The man who was laughing."

"Laughing?"

A startled look was on the youngster's face.

"I assure you the man is unsafe. He has already used his knife to me in a way which proves that he would stick at nothing. Where is he?"

I stood up to see. As I did so an observation was made by a person who was sitting some little distance down the table on the opposite side.

"I don't fancy the gentleman can be quite well. If he will take the advice of a medical man—I happen to be a medical man—I think that he had better retire to his own apartment."

I was nettled at this.

"I am obliged to you, sir, but I happen to be in the enjoyment of perfect health. I don't think it is unreasonable to suggest that the sound of that man's laughter is calculated to unsettle the strongest nerves."

"But I heard no laughter."

This was said by an elderly gentleman who was seated next to the person who asserted that he was a medical man.

"In that case I congratulate you. Your hearing, sir, must be dulled. I should say that you are the only person in the room who didn't. I can only hope that it won't occur again."

"I hope it won't."

This was from the youngster on my right. There was on his face a look which I did not like. On second thoughts I perceived that he was not moved so much by terror as by a desire to smile. I returned to the consideration of my fish. I was aware that I had created a small sensation. I was also aware that my wife was endeavouring to conceal the fact that she was crying at my side. Before, however, I could find words with which to quiet her, the stranger, leaning across the table, whispered—

"He is back again!"

Down went my knife and fork with something, I fancy, of a clatter.

"Are you sure?"

"Look for yourself and see."

I sprang to my feet. I searched eagerly round the room. As I rose the young fellow on my right rose with me.

"Steady, old man! Don't you think you had better take it easy and sit down?"

He was speaking to me as if I were a child. But at that moment I caught sight of the scoundrel leaning with his back against the wall.

"Look at him! Do you see his knife? I ask you if such a fellow ought to be allowed in the dining-room of a respectable hotel?"

"Certainly not, but they will get in sometimes, don't you know. Now sit down, do."

The youngster was still talking to me as if I were a child; he even laid his hand upon my shoulder. Twisting myself free, I fixed on him a glance which caused him to shrink a little back.

"Be so good, sir, as to remove your hand. If you suppose that I am a person with whom you may take liberties you are under a singular delusion. I am a resident in this hotel, and as such I have a right to object to the presence of improper characters. That man there—I can see you! it is no good your dodging behind the waiter!—has been annoying me for a good time. He has been coming and going in a way which will end in making me quite ill. I intend to submit to it no longer; I insist on his removal."

Many of the diners had risen from the table. The room was in confusion. An old lady exclaimed—

"What is the matter with the man? Is he mad?"

Another old woman replied, speaking behind her hand, but I heard her, in spite of the precautions which she took to prevent me—

"Drink, my dear!"

Someone cried, "Mad as a March hare!"

I faced the speakers.

"I regret that any here should think it necessary to insult me. I expected, instead of insult, your support. Surely there is none here who can say that such a man as that is a fit person to be amongst us."

"Raymond," cried my wife, "come away with me. Do come!"

"What is the use of that? He is sure to follow me."

"I shouldn't be surprised; they do do that at times."

This was from the youngster on my right. A waiter advanced.

"Come this way, sir."

"Pray, why?"

"I think you'd better."

The man's tone was actually cajoling.

"Do you indeed? I think you had better do your duty and remove that man."

"What man, sir? I don't see no man."

"Don't you see no man? I allude to that man there with no hat on, and with the butcher's knife in his hand."

The waiter shrank away.

"I—I don't know what you're talking of; I—I shouldn't think, sir, as you was well."

The man was too insignificant to bandy words with.

"Bring me the landlord!" I demanded.

"Here is the landlord coming."

He was; he advanced towards me up the room.

"Landlord, you appear to harbour some very curious characters in your hotel. You see that man there with the butcher's knife? he has been annoying me for the last hour and more. He has already tried to murder me. Before he actually commits a crime I insist on his removal."

"He shall be removed at once. You had better come with me. They will have more difficulty in removing him while you are here."

"Why should that be? Am I not to remain because such a villain as that wishes to drive me out?"

"He's a very dangerous character; he's often here. Come along."

"How dare you try to take my arm! Then if he is often here the fact should be widely known, and you should be prevented from receiving respectable people as your guests. Stand aside, sir! remove your hand! See, he's coming!"

I fancy the landlord was a little taken by surprise by the way in which I whirled him round.

"There, he's got upon the table!"

The scoundrel had, right among the plates and dishes.

"Let me get at him! I'll soon put him off again, knife or no knife."

I began to climb on the table.

"Now then, look what he's doing! Catch hold of him, some of you." I imagined that the landlord's words referred to the scoundrel who was playing his antics among the plates and dishes; but, to my surprise, they referred to me. At least, I presume so, for, simultaneously, half a dozen persons caught me by the shoulders. I thrust them from me with an effort of strength of which I had not thought I was capable. At the same instant the man sat upon the table, and leaping over their heads, landed on the floor.

"Here he is! Stand back!" I cried.

They stood back, hustling each other in a way which was almost comical. I addressed the individual who was the cause of all the tumult.

"Now, you scamp, I will try conclusions with you. No one else seems disposed to do so, so I will take that office on myself. Out you go."

I advanced to him. He did not flinch. He raised his knife threateningly in the air. But I did not care for that. Running in, I caught him round the waist. I lifted him from his feet. He wound his arms about me. He was strong, but I myself am not a weakling. We struggled furiously. Finding that I could not throw him, I slipped my right hand upwards and caught him with it by the throat. In my rage I was half inclined to choke the life out of him. I could have done it! But, as I compressed my grasp, without an instant's warning he was gone! I was struggling with a phantom! There was nothing there!

"He is gone!" I exclaimed, looking about to see if there were traces of him left.

"Quite time he was gone." This, I knew, came from the youth who had been sitting on my right. "If he had not gone I should."

"Now then, catch hold of him before he has another attack. But don't use any more force than you can help."

Incredible though it may seem, the landlord was urging on the waiters to attack me. But before they could realise the atrocity of their employer's requirements the stranger interposed.

"Excuse me, but I think that this is a case with which I had better deal. Will you kindly, for one moment, leave this gentleman to me?"

"They had better," I declared. "You seem to be the only sane man here. Anybody would think that in this hotel ruffians with butchers' knives were not only allowed, but encouraged to do exactly as they please."

"Look me in the eyes." I did so, though I certainly did not know why. "Now then! Presto! Bang!"

I don't know what he did. He did something. It seemed to me that he raised his hand and snapped his fingers in the air. That same second something happened to me, though I really don't know what. A great weight seemed lifted from me; my brain seemed all at once to clear. It was as though I had escaped from the toils of some horrid nightmare, as though I had woke all at once from sleep. I looked about me with awakening eyes. I knew that I had been an actor in some sort of dreadful dream. There were the people gathered round. There was the stranger standing just in front of me. He had a slight smile upon his lips. He thrust his hand into the breast-pocket of his coat.

"Ladies and gentlemen, allow me to introduce myself."

He produced a folded paper. Unfolding it, he held it up before their eyes. It was a placard, printed in alternative lines of black and red.

"Signor Segundi, the world-renowned prestidigitateur, begs to announce that he will give his celebrated entertainment."

It ran in some such fashion. It was an advertisement of an entertainment of "magic and mystery" to be given at the Assembly Rooms that very night. The stranger placed his hand against his breast and bowed. "Ladies and gentlemen, I am Signor Segundi, wholly at your service. It has occurred to me that I might vary my little programme with the addition of some slight novelty. Hypnotism, as you are aware, is, as they put it, all the rage. Was it not possible to give my programme a scientific turn? Unfortunately, I am no hypnotist. With the best intentions in the world I have only been able to perform a few experiments upon my wife. In these matters an artist's wife is regarded with suspicion by the public eye. About an hour ago I entered the room upstairs. I found this gentleman seated in it all alone. Something told me that chance, that unknown quantity, had all at once, so to speak, thrown a subject at my head. The true artist is he who grasps at opportunities. I grasped at mine, and, if I may say so, for the moment was inspired. I told a story about a ghost—a most mysterious ghost—which I met upon the road to Goring. As I proceeded with my narrative I found, to my astonishment, that the subject was being hypnotised before I was myself aware of it. We had a most charming little entertainment, quite between ourselves and entirely in private. We have had, as you have seen, an equally charming little entertainment of a more public kind. Ladies and gentlemen, I have to thank you for your kind attention to that portion of our programme which is now concluded."

The fellow bowed—and ceased. I gasped. He had made of me a laughing-stock—a live advertisement! He turned to me.

"I have to tender you my heartiest thanks, sir, for the generous assistance you have rendered, and which has made the experiment so entirely successful."

I endeavoured to restrain myself.

"I hope you will consider it equally successful by the time I've finished."

He would have done if they had let me get at him. But Oates and my wife and others intervened. I am not a Bombastes Furioso. I am not, as a rule, a fighting man. But if they had allowed me to get within the reach of that impostor, he should have had as successful a five minutes' entertainment as he ever enjoyed. As it was, they got him out of the room by one door, and me out of it by another.

"It seems to me," I observed to my wife, when she and I were alone together, "that if one man is allowed to play hanky-panky with another man, not only against his will, but actually without his knowledge, the liberty of the subject promises to grow smaller by degrees and beautifully less."

My wife agreed with me.

"I thought you were mad," she said.

"I am mad; but I will make him madder before I've done."

So I will. I intend to keep a keen look-out for Signor Segundi's "Celebrated Entertainment." When I hear of its being about to take place, I mean to form one of the audience and try on the Signor a little experiment planned and carried out on lines of my own. I hope it will be as successful as his was.

Pourquoipas

I. The Talking Horse

"But, madame, I do not understand you!"

"It is a mystery!"

"A mystery!" Mr. Fletcher felt that the word inadequately described the situation. "Do you mean to say—I hardly know whether to take you seriously—that you have been having a conversation with a horse?"

"That is to say, with my husband—with Ernest."

"I thought you said that he was dead?"

"It is certain. Did I not see him die? I will show you the bed upon which we laid him out. Did I not shed upon his corpse my tears? What would you have?"

"Then how about the conversation?"

"It is metempsychosis."

Mr. Fletcher began to be amused.

"Metempsychosis?"

"It is a theory of which I know but little. Is it an article of faith with which monsieur is acquainted?"

"Not much—personally."

"I? I am a Catholic. Ernest? He was I know not what! These men! Never shall I forget my feelings when—when I suggested sending for a priest; he said that it was not worth while to trouble the good man, for when he died his soul would pass into a horse."

"A horse?"

"A horse! He even named the horse! It is incredible!"

Mr. Fletcher thought it was—almost.

"Monsieur must know that my husband—he is dead, what does it matter?—was not to me a good husband. I did my best to bring him to a sense of what was right, of what was proper; but, after all, it is little that a wife can do, is it not so? He had his little fortune, I had mine. Puff! before I knew it, his was gone. Do not ask me how. He would have sent mine with it; I said no. He was a great horseman. He used to keep horses to run at races, and to sell—that was his business; the hotel was mine—and among them was the famous Pourquoipas—all the world has heard of Pourquoipas."

All the world might have done. Mr. Fletcher had not. He said so.

"Monsieur has not heard of Pourquoipas! It is extraordinary! He is the greatest trotting horse in the world. It is little I know of these things, but I do know that Pourquoipas is indeed a marvel. He was my horse, as indeed, when you have the truth, were all the others. Judge, then, of my surprise when, as I told monsieur, I said to Ernest, 'Shall I send for a priest?' he replied, 'Of what use? When I die my soul will pass into Pourquoipas.' 'What nonsense are you talking?' I demanded. 'Agnes,' he said, 'you have often accused me of having no religion. I have a religion. I believe in the doctrine of metempsychosis.' 'What horror is that?' I cried. 'It is the doctrine of transmigration of souls. I am now about to die. I believe that when I am dead my soul will pass into the body of Pourquoipas. It is as I say. Those who live longest will see most.' He looked at me with his glassy eyes. He turned over on his side. Before I knew it he was dead. Those were nice last words for a wife to hear from a husband as he was entering the grave.

"I said nothing to anyone. I was too much ashamed. The day before yesterday he was buried. Yesterday morning I entered the stable to see that all was well. I was looking at Pourquoipas. I was wondering what I should do with him. He is entered for half a dozen races—and what do I know of racing?—and suddenly Pourquoipas turned and looked at me. 'Agnes,' he said, 'good-day.' Monsieur, it was my husband's voice. I fell to the ground. They found me in a fit. They carried me to the house. Oh, mon Dieu!"

The lady applied her handkerchief to her eyes. Apparently she wept.

"Don't you think it possible," suggested Mr. Fletcher mildly, "that you were the victim of a delusion?"

"Possible. When I returned to consciousness I said to myself, 'It is sure! I am no fool—I!' The more I thought of it the more I said to myself it was a trick my fancy played me. Last night when I went to bed this idea was clearly presented to my mind."

Madame Peltier paused. She glanced round the room with what was very like a glance of apprehension.

"Monsieur, last night I had no doubt upon the matter. This morning I found, pinned to my pillow, a piece of paper, on which was written the words, 'Come to the stable.' They were in my husband's hand-writing. I have the piece of paper in my pocket."

She rummaged in a pocket, which seemed as remarkable for the variety of its contents as any schoolboy's could possibly have been. Finally she produced a scrap of paper; this she placed upon the table with a flourish which was essentially dramatic.

"There it is; monsieur may see it for himself."

It was a quarter-sheet of dirty note-paper, on which was written, in a cramped French handwriting, the words, "Come to the stable."

"It is my husband's handwriting; there are a hundred persons who can swear to it. I said, 'It is another trick.' But, in spite of myself, I went to the stable. Scarcely had I put my foot inside the door than Pourquoipas looked round to me with this remark, 'You see, my wife, it is as I said.'"

"Did you have another fit?"

"Would that I had! It was not all he said, not by a great deal. He advised me to commit suicide."

"In order to join him in the bosom of Pourquoipas?"

"Not actually, but in effect. He desired, the vagabond! that I should ruin myself. He said that I was to send all the horses and a sum of money—ah! what a sum!—to an address at Morlaix. I was to ask no questions as to their destination; I was to dismiss them from my mind as though they had never been."

Mr. Fletcher rose from his seat.

"You don't mean that he said all that?"

"It is the truth. All the horses and ten thousand francs—all to be sent to a man at Morlaix, of whom I had never heard. It would be my ruin; as well commit suicide at once."

"This gets interesting."

"He said that if I did not do it he would haunt me by day and by night; he would make my life a burden; he would make me wish that I was never born."

"Seriously, madame, are you quite sure that you were not again the victim of your own imagination?"

"I have no imagination; I know not what it is. When I hear a thing, I hear a thing; and when I hear my husband's voice I know it, monsieur may rest assured of that. Besides, there is the paper."

There was the paper, but Mr. Fletcher did not see that there was much in that. Oddly enough, he had been routing out materials for an article on Breton superstitions, when he stumbled on this find at Plestin. He had not been in the place half a dozen hours when the landlady of his hotel, "La Boule d'Or," thrust on him her confidence. She said—he had never had such an accusation hurled at him before—that "monsieur looked so sympathetic."

On the shore he found the stables. They were built within a stone's-throw of the sea. Outwardly, they had not the appearance of a typical training stable—of a training stable, that is, as it is known in England. A lank, knock-kneed individual was lounging in front of the door, who was the typical English jockey as he is found in fifth-rate racing establishments in "foreign parts." Him Mr. Fletcher accosted.

"Got some decent horses, I hear."

The "jockey" looked him up and down.

"They've got four legs most on 'em."

Mr. Fletcher knew that the speaker had already read his inmost soul, and was aware that his equine knowledge extended no further than the capability of being able to draw a distinction between a horse and an ass.

"Four good legs some of them, I understand."

"About as good as yours and mine."

Mr. Fletcher felt that this language, in one in the position of the speaker, was out of place.

"Can I have a peep at them?"

"There's no law again' it, as I knows on."

The stable door was open; Mr. Fletcher entered. The jockey slouched in after him. The arrangements were primitive, but the building was of considerable size, and some eight or nine animals were in the boxes.

"Which is Pourquoipas?"

"That is Pourquoipas." On Mr. Fletcher moving towards the animal indicated the jockey was moved to further eloquence. "He is a 'orse, he is." Pause. "He is a 'orse." Another pause. "There ain't no trotter like him, not in Europe, there ain't. I ought to know." Pause. "And I says so." Pause. "That 'orse can do his mile inside of two-eleven." The speaker glanced at Mr. Fletcher, as if challenging contradiction; but as that gentleman was unaware of there being anything remarkable in a horse "doing his mile inside of two-eleven" his countenance was blank. "Yes, and inside of two-ten, if he's fairly on the job."

Again a look in the nature of a challenge; still no reply. In possible disgust the jockey did what Mr. Fletcher was hoping he would do—he turned on his heels and left the stable. He seemed to see nothing surprising in leaving a perfect stranger to examine the stud at his leisure.

Mr. Fletcher was content, however, to confine his attention to one member of the stud—to Pourquoipas.

"So you're Pourquoipas, are you? I don't know much about the genus trotting horse, but if you're a fair example of the rest of your tribe you're not a handsome family. Big, gawky, leggy brute! You look to me more like a cart-horse gone wrong than any other kind of quadruped I've seen!" Pourquoipas looked round with sullen eyes, as though he resented these observations of a too candid critic.

"A nice sort of man the late Peltier must have been to have wished to transfer his soul to such a thing of beauty as yourself."

The creature made a movement with his hind legs, which caused Mr. Fletcher to nimbly step aside.

"Now then, whose toes are you trying to step upon? A pretty mean sort of scamp your master must have been."

There ensued an interval of silence. Mr. Fletcher stared at the horse, and the horse at him. It was a stare, perhaps, of mutual admiration.

"Fat English pig!"

It was these words, spoken in French, which broke that interval of silence. Mr. Fletcher started back in so much haste as to come into sudden and unexpected contact with the stable wall. It seemed that this flattering address proceeded from Pourquoipas! For some seconds he gazed at the animal with an astonishment which was altogether unequivocal.

"I'm not surprised that it frightened the woman! The thing was uncommonly well done. Now, my ventriloquial friend, where are you?"

Echo answered where. Mr. Fletcher treated Pourquoipas with very little ceremony. He drove him from side to side of his box, so that no corner of it was hidden. He peered into his manger; he routed among the straw; he looked up at the ceiling; he examined the other boxes—there was nothing there but horses. He returned to stare at Pourquoipas; and the more he stared the more the wonder grew.

"Blockhead."

The same voice; and again it seemed to proceed from Pourquoipas.

"So there was something in it after all. I thought the woman was romancing. Well, this is something new in travellers' tales. I wonder, my friend, just where you are?"

While he wondered the voice went on—

"You think, you English, that you are wise. Bah! You are a nation of fools! Go back to your land of fogs; there you will be more at home than here."

"Is that all?" asked Mr. Fletcher, when the voice was still.

It seemed that it was. All efforts on his part to provoke a continuation of the conversation proved futile. His language was not exactly choice, his allusions were not entirely civil; but nothing he could say had any effect upon the quadruped, or upon the gentleman behind the scenes who had endowed the quadruped, pro tem., with the faculty of speech.

"If the seance is concluded I suppose I'd better go."

As he left the stable he told himself—

"Unless I am mistaken, our friend the jockey has a finger in this pie."

When he got into the open air the first thing he saw was the jockey, walking beside a horse which a lad was exercising on the sands a good three-quarters of a mile away.

Later on Mr. Fletcher, having returned to the hotel for dinner, noticed above the mantelpiece of the salle-a-manger the picture of a man. The portrait was in oils, and life-size. The man was leaning over a table, staring the spectator in the face. It was in the modern style of French sensation—the man seemed actually alive! But, in its way, it was distinctly a work of art. Mr. Fletcher asked the Breton maid, who brought in his soup, who the original was.

"It is the patron the husband of madame. It is a good likeness. But, for me, I do not like it. Whenever I look at it I think that he is going to leap at me across the table."

The idea was not inapt; he did look as though he were about to spring.

"Wasn't he a little man?"

"But a dwarf. That is how he was so good a rider."

The face in the picture was not an evil face. It seemed to Mr. Fletcher that it was rather the face of a fool than a knave. But about the whole portrait there was a curious appearance of life—one momentarily expected the man to spring.

That night Mr. Fletcher was aroused from his first sleep by a tapping at his bedroom door. At first—as we are apt to do—he wondered what it was that had disturbed his slumber. Tap, tap, tap! As he listened there came a further tapping at the panel of the door. He started up in bed.

"Who's there?"

"Open, monsieur, for the love of heaven."

It was a woman's voice.

"Is that you, madame?"

"Open, monsieur. I pray you, open."

"What's the matter?"

Slipping into a pair of trousers, Mr. Fletcher went to see. Outside the door was Madame Peltier in a costume of the most amazing scantiness.

She had a lighted candle in her hand. Without waiting for an invitation, pushing past the gentleman, she entered his room. Putting her candle on the table, herself she placed upon a chair. Mr. Fletcher felt that this behaviour of his landlady's required an explanation, even in the wilds of Côtes du Nord!

"May I ask, madame, what is wrong?"

Now that she had gained admittance, the lady appeared to be in a state of speechless agitation; it was plain that there was something wrong.

"Ernest!" she gasped. "Ernest! I have seen him."

"Ernest?" For a moment the name conveyed no significance to Mr. Fletcher's bewildered brain. "You mean your husband?"

"My husband! I have seen his ghost!"

"His ghost?"

Mr. Fletcher was becoming conscious that there might be more excitement in the country than in the town.

"I have seen his ghost; oh, mon Dieu! I was asleep. Suddenly I awoke. Someone was leaning over me, having a tight hold of my arm. It was Ernest. Oh, mon Dieu!"

"You were dreaming."

"Dreaming! I wish I had been dreaming. Is that a dream?" The lady pulled up the sleeve of her single garment. An ugly bruise showed on the skin of her plump, white arm. "Ernest was a little man, but he had a wrist like steel. That is where he gripped me. Is that a dream?"

"How do you know it was your husband?"

"Do I not know my husband? He whispered in my ear—oh, the horror! 'You see, my wife, it is as I said.' I was too frightened to speak. 'I will haunt you by day and night until you do my bidding.' Then he began again about the horses and the ten thousand francs which I am to send to a Monsieur Quelquechose at Morlaix—just as I heard it, every word, from Pourquoipas. It will be my ruin!"

While the lady sobbed, Mr. Fletcher, in his unstockinged feet, paced to and fro.

"It strikes me that there is some plot on foot to deprive you of your property. Do you know anything about that jockey of yours?"

"Sam Tucker? He is a fool, and a knave. What then?"

"Do you think him capable of originating an elaborate scheme of robbery?"

"He is capable of anything; he is always robbing me. What has that to do with my husband?"

"That, at present, is more than I can tell you. Of course, the ghostly visitation was a trick."

"Is that a trick?"

The lady pointed to the bruise upon her arm.

"That is part of the trick. But I will talk the matter over with you in the morning, and we will see what can be done. You had better return to your room. You are hardly likely to receive another visit from that very versatile husband of yours to-night."

"I would not return to my room—not for ten thousand horses and a million francs."

"Then you had better go to your maid. I suppose that you hardly propose remaining here?"

The lady went to her maid. Immediately on her departure the gentleman turned into bed. But he could not sleep; he turned, and tossed, and tumbled; the lady's visit had banished slumber. Pourquoipas, the words which had fallen—or which had seemed to fall—from the creature's lips, the lady's story—half a dozen things were jumbled together in his mind.

Perhaps some twenty minutes or half an hour had elapsed since the lady had gone. He was lying on his left side, with his face turned towards the wall. His eyes were closed, in the forlorn hope that sleep would come upon them unawares. But as he lay, and no sleep came, and, instead, phantoms of thought persisted in chasing each other across his brain, in weariness of spirit he opened them to look out upon the world.

As he did so he was surprised to see that a light—a faint light—was shining on the wall. His first impression was that it was later than he had imagined, and that the first glimmerings of daylight were finding their way into the room. Something, however, in the colour of the light suggested that it certainly was not daylight. And, as he lay in a sort of drowsy stupor, his eyes still fixed on the dimly illuminated wall, he began to fear that that absurd woman had returned, to outrage the proprieties, and to seek shelter from her fears.

"Confound her! If this isn't something like an hotel, I never knew one yet! Talk about travellers being taken in and done for!"

This he muttered beneath his breath. Then he turned lazily in bed, intending, with as much politeness as circumstances would permit, to call down execrations on his hostess. But he did not call down execrations on his hostess, because his hostess was not there.

When he turned in bed he perceived that the room was lighted, but from what source there was no evidence to show. The light was, so to speak, just enough to cast the room in shadow; just enough to make things visible, and yet not plain. It was a dim and a ghostly light.

While Mr. Fletcher was wondering to what unseen friend he was indebted for this genteel illumination, all at once his eyes fell upon a man, who was standing on the other side of the table, leaning over the board. He could have sworn that he was not there when he first had turned, a second ago, for his glance had travelled all round the room, in search of his landlady, and he had seen that it was empty. Yet it was equally certain that now the man was there, unless, that is, he was the victim of an hallucination. When one is awake, and in one's right mind, one does not, as a general rule, see things which are non-existent; and now he saw that man.

He was a very little man, if that was any consolation, and he was a curious-looking little man. As he leaned across the table his attitude conveyed an odd and slightly uncanny impression of his being about to spring. There was silence. The visitor made no remark. Mr. Fletcher, on his part, made none. The man was a stranger to him, and yet—where had he seen him before? Suddenly he remembered—in the picture over the mantelpiece in the salle-a-manger. He was the patron the husband of madame! Either the artist had caught, in a marvellous and prophetic manner, his sitter's pose, or the sitter had caught the artist's inspiration. Mr. Fletcher saw the picture reproduced before his eyes, as in the portrait—the little man looked as though he were going to leap at him across the table!

"Monsieur, a little of your attention."

The visitor opened the ball of conversation the voice was the voice which had seemed to proceed from Pourquoipas.

"You are an Englishman? Very good. Confine yourself to your own affairs. Return to your own country."

The visitor's manner was distinctly acid. As he listened, Mr. Fletcher became very certain that the man in front of him was neither a spectre of his own imagination, nor a visitant from shadowland.

"You hear? I say, return to your own country."

Mr. Fletcher heard, and, as he heard, he sat up in bed and contemplated the speaker at his leisure.

"You're a nice young man, upon my word!"

This form of reply seemed to take the visitor aback. He seemed to think that he had not created a sufficient impression.

"You do not know who I am?"

"Oh, yes I do, thanks."

"You think I am alive?"

"I don't think you are."

"Very good. Try and see." The speaker raised his hand, with a little mocking gesture. "But I warn you to take care. Above all, I warn you not to meddle in affairs which are no concern of yours. Go away from here, or—you will regret it."

"I assure you, honestly, that I shall not regret it if remaining here will afford me an opportunity of having frequent interviews with you. You are the sort of man, I should say, who improves upon acquaintance."

"You laugh at me? Well, you will not laugh long. I warn you to go away from here before tomorrow night, or you will be sorry."

"Sorry? Not at all! You little brute!"

As Mr. Fletcher uttered this last exclamation, springing out of bed, he bounded to-wards the little man behind the table. He moved with great agility, but if he expected to take the other by surprise he failed. No sooner did his feet touch the floor than the mysterious light vanished, and, despite his haste, all that he succeeded in doing was to come in violent contact with the table.

Some strongish language escaped his lips as, in the pitchy darkness, he went rushing round the table. He succeeded in reaching the other side of it; he also succeeded, when he reached it, in finding nothing there.

"Where are you, you hound?"

No voice replied. He stood a moment, listening. There was not a sound.

"I know you're somewhere in the room. Only wait until I lay my hands on you!"

Even as he spoke someone laid a hand on him, lightly, on his arm; and a voice—a well-known voice—observed—

"Good-night, dear friend—until tomorrow!"

Mr, Fletcher sprang round with an agility which was really marvellous, grasping wildly at the speaker. He grasped, however, nothing but the air. When he realised that there was nothing there to grasp, Mr. Fletcher's language was quite unprintable. At last he lit the candle. By its glimmer he examined the room—there was nothing but the room to examine. All traces of his visitor had disappeared. Nor could he find anything which went to show the means by which that disappearance had been effected. The door was locked, so was the window.

"Where has the little beggar gone? It strikes me that this is quite a model thing in hotels. It dates from before the flood; and I'll stake a pound it's honeycombed with sliding doors and secret passages, like the hotels used to be in the good old-fashioned tales of my boyhood."

As he came to this conclusion he returned to the table behind which the little man had stood. His eyes fell upon a piece of paper which was lying in its centre.

"What is that? I didn't notice anything there when I lit the candle."

It was a quarter-sheet of dirty notepaper—own brother to the scrap which Madame had shown him. It contained two words, written in the same cramped handwriting as the words upon her piece—

"Until tomorrow."

"That's odd. How came that there? There can be no doubt that the thing's well done."

He thought so when, having put out the candle and returned into bed, on laying his head on the pillow, his cheek came into contact with another scrap of paper.

"What the—!"

He sprang out of bed as though a serpent had stung him. With hands which actually trembled he once more caused light to shine upon the scene. He bore the candle to the bed—sure enough there was a piece of paper on the pillow.

"How in thunder did that get there?"

As gingerly as though it were some precious or, perhaps, some deadly thing, he picked it up between his finger and his thumb. It was the third of the series—another dirty quarter-sheet; and on it, in the old, familiar hand, was this excellent advice: "Do not meddle with the affairs of others." The advice was excellent; there could be no doubt of that. But still Mr. Fletcher felt that its excellence did not sufficiently account for its presence on his pillow. This time, when he returned into bed, he did not put the candle out. He left it burning.

Sleep has been compared to a woman—"uncertain, coy, and hard to please." When we seek for slumber it eludes us; when we least expect it, behold, it comes! It came to Mr. Fletcher then. Hardly was he once more between the sheets before he was sleeping softly as a child.

II. The Living Picture

When Mr. Fletcher awoke—there was no mistake about it this time—it was broad day. He lay for some moments revelling in the first joy of waking. When he thought of the events of the night he laughed aloud; they were so utterly absurd. Remembering the scraps of paper he sat up in bed to look for them. In rising his glance fell upon his pillow; there, on the snowy linen, within half an inch of where his cheek had just been resting, branded, as it seemed, in blood, was the impress of a horse's hoof.

Mr. Fletcher managed, during the early portion of that day, to avoid his hostess. He went out into the village. There appeared to be only one shop in the place; at the door of that establishment stood a man. He was a big, burly fellow in blouse and sabots; he looked a companionable soul. Mr. Fletcher found him what he looked—a gossip. Mr. Fletcher began by alluding to the natural beauties of the neighbourhood; he then remarked that he was staying at "La Boule d'Or," the landlord of which, he understood, had lately died.

"It was time he did."

"Such a scamp, was he?"

"As honest a man as ever lived."

Mr. Fletcher pricked up his ears at this.

"Rather wild, wasn't he?"

"There never was a quieter soul."

"But wasn't he extravagant?"

"Extravagant! For example, he had never a sou to spend."

"That, I suppose, was after he had spent all he had to spend?"

Monsieur Bonchard—the name was painted on the little window over his door—cast at Mr. Fletcher a contemplative glance; he placed his hands on the upper portion of his capacious stomach.

"I see."

"What do you see?"

"You have been listening to Madame Peltier."

"Madame Peltier certainly gave me to understand that he was not all a husband should have been."

"Marie!" Monsieur Bonchard called into the shop. A feminine reproduction of himself came towards the front. "What sort of a husband was Peltier up at the 'Hotel de la Boule d'Or'?"

"A model husband—a true model."

"As for his wife—"

The lady interposed.

"It is not for us to say anything."

"I was his friend; it is for me to say the truth. She murdered him!"

"Murdered him!"

Mr. Fletcher felt that the authorities were too conflicting.

"Not with a pistol and a knife, but with her cruelty. She led him the life of a dog! She did not let him have enough to eat; she would not let him have a sou to call his own; she would not let him have his liberty; she used to lock him up in a room for days; she beat him."

"Beat him!"

"Never shall I forget one night he came to me; he was crying—ah! like my little baby. 'Bonchard,' he said, 'it is finished. She has beaten me!'"

"With her shoe," explained the lady, "as though he were a little child."

"He was a very little man; she was a big woman; he was as nothing in her hands. She used to say she would show him as a dwarf. Ah, what he suffered! He had a spirit which was too large for his body. After that beating—monsieur, he was black and blue, with my own eyes I saw the bruises!—within a week he was no more—he was dead. That is why I say she murdered him."

"One tale is good," reflected Mr. Fletcher, "until another is told. The fault does not appear to have been all upon one side. If she beat him with her shoe—degradation not to be surpassed—I don't wonder that he preferred the bosom of Pourquoipas."

Corroboration of Monsieur Bonchard's story was obtained from another quarter—from the Breton maid who waited upon him at his midday meal.

"What sort of man was the late Monsieur Peltier?"

"An angel."

Mr. Fletcher felt that this was strong. The maid did not look as though she was an enthusiastic damsel. On the other hand, still less did Monsieur Peltier—in his portrait—look as though he were an angel.

"What was there angelic about him?"

"He was so good; that was his fault—he was too good. He was a little man—such a little man—one could have nursed him like a baby."

Mr. Fletcher was conscious that there might be drawbacks in being nursed like a baby.

"I suppose, then, that he and his wife lived happily together?"

"Happily! Ah, for example!" The damsel was standing by his chair. Stooping, she whispered in his ear: "Madame has a tongue!" Standing up, she looked about her, possibly to see if the coast was clear: "And madame has an arm! You see that?" She pointed to a red mark upon her cheek. "She has just done it. She may be big, but I will let her know that next time she slaps me it shall not be for nothing."

It was possible that the damsel's evidence was prejudiced. When one has just been slapped, one does not necessarily have a high opinion of the slapper. Still, straws show which way the wind is blowing. It was evident that public opinion was not unanimous in reprobating Monsieur Peltier.

Mr. Fletcher did not see his hostess until after supper. He was quitting the salle-a-manger when he heard the sound of sobbing. The sound proceeded from a little room at the foot of the stairs. The door of the room was open. In it was Madame Peltier.

"Monsieur, I entreat you, enter."

Mr. Fletcher entered.

"It is all over. It is done. It is finished."

Mr. Fletcher inquired what was finished.

"I am ruined. It is of no consequence to anyone—that I know very well—but it is all the world to me."

Mr. Fletcher asked—being driven upon the paths of cross-examination—in what way she was ruined.

"I have just given orders that all my horses—Pourquoipas alone is worth five-and-twenty thousand francs—and all the money I have in the world are to be sent to a man in Morlaix, of whom I have not even heard the name."

"You are not serious?"

"Do I look as though I were not serious, monsieur? What would you have? Ask Sam Tucker. He is going to take both the money and the horses."

"If you really have given such an order I would earnestly advise you to countermand it. You don't mean to say, now you have had an opportunity for quiet thought, that you are not yourself persuaded that you have been the victim of a trick?"

"What do you call a trick? Was that a trick last night? Do not tell me I do not know my own husband, if you please. All this morning I say to myself, 'I will go into the stable. No, no, no!' This afternoon I find upon my table a piece of paper—'Come!' Who put it there? It is in my husband's writing. I went to the stable, although I said to myself I would not go. I have heard there from Pourquoipas—ah! what I have heard! Never was I spoken to in such a way before; and by a horse! Ciel! It is a wonder I am not dead! It is enough that I promised to send the horses and the money, by Sam Tucker, to a man at Morlaix, whose name even I do not know."

"I would strongly advise you to put off the fulfilment of your promise—at any rate, until the morning."

"It is impossible! I am not a woman without courage, but I do not dare."

She did dare. Mr. Fletcher persuaded her. The sacrifice was postponed.

"Now," the gentleman told himself, "unless I am greatly mistaken, to-night I shall have another visitor as the consequence of meddling with the affairs of others!"

His forebodings were realised—he had a visitor! He put off retiring to the latest possible moment. When he did seek the privacy of his own apartment, he still postponed the act of going to bed.

"I think I remember seeing somewhere a little play called Diamond Cut Diamond. If I am to receive a visit I think I'll receive him sitting up. I shall be able to offer him more courtesy than I should if I were in bed."

He put out the candle, taking care to have it within easy reach. He put a box of matches in his pocket, only regretting that there was no lantern handy. Taking off his boots, he sat down in a chair and waited. He waited hours. Nothing broke the silence of the night; no church clock told of the flight of time.

"One might almost think that someone had told my friend that I had a six-shooter in my pocket, the better to do him honour. If something doesn't happen soon I shall either have to walk about or else go to sleep in my chair; and if it comes to that, I 'd better go to bed."

The night stole on. Still nothing to break the monotony of waiting in the dark. More than once Mr. Fletcher had caught his chin in the act of falling forward on to his chest—his yawns became prodigious!

"It begins to occur to me that, at my time of life, nothing and no one is worth sitting up for all night. I'm off to bed."

He was about to go to bed, and, for that purpose, had already risen from his seat, when—he heard a sound!

"What's that?"

It might have been the creaking of a board; it might have been the movement of a mouse; it might have been any of the trifling noises of which we are conscious in the silence of the night. Of one thing only he was certain—he had heard a sound! He listened, his sense of hearing almost unnaturally alert. A sound again!

"Perhaps, after all, it's nothing but a mouse."

If it was a mouse, it was a curious one. The sound became plainer. It seemed to Mr. Fletcher that it was coming nearer.

"It's someone moving. I hope to goodness it isn't that old idiot, madame."

But it did not seem as if it proceeded from the stairs. Surely, if she came at all, she would come that way.

"It strikes me that it is someone in the other room. For all I know there may be someone sleeping there. Halloa! what's that?"

It was a ray of light—the merest pencil; it gleamed, like a streak of molten metal, across the floor.

"As I'm a Dutchman it's shining through the wall!"

It was, there could be no doubt of it; it came through a crevice in the wainscot.

"I have it! I spot it all! Now for the next card in the game it'll be a call for trumps. I rather fancy, too, that I shall be able to trump this little trick."

The pencil of light grew wider.

"They're slipping a panel in the wainscot—just behind the head of my bed! This thing gets beautifully plain."

With a cat-like step Mr. Fletcher moved towards the bed. The pencil of light was ceasing to be a pencil—it began to illuminate the room.

"Steady, my friend, that panel distinctly creaked; you must oil it next time before you play this game. In delicate operations of this kind ' trifles light as air ' are apt to spoil the full effect."

The room was in that state of semi-radiance which had puzzled Mr. Fletcher on the previous night.

"Now, my friend, is it now? It is! He's coming. Trumped! Good —evening, dear friend, good-evening."

With one hand he had someone by the collar of his coat, with the other he pointed a revolver into someone's face."

"Good-evening, dear friend, good-evening."

There ensued an interval for reflection. The captive seemed momentarily paralysed; the captor was taking stock. The prisoner was a little man—a very little man, scarcely reaching above Mr. Fletcher's waist.

"After all!"

The words proceeded from the little man in something between a moan and a gasp.

"As you say, my friend, 'after all'—after all we meet again. Perhaps you will permit me to strike a light—my light? Your light we will examine later on."

The little man offered no resistance when his captor drew him towards the table. He stood in silence while the candle was being lit, nor did he flinch when Mr. Fletcher held it in front of his face, the better to see what manner of man he was.

"From the look of you I should say you were the late Peltier's Corsican brother."

"You have a revolver; shoot me, it is better so."

"It may be better so—a little later in the evening; at the present it seems to me that it would be a pity. Let me place you on the table."

Lifting him in his arms Mr. Fletcher seated him on the edge of the table, the little man remaining as docile as a child. When, however, he had gained that post of vantage, "What it is to have been born a little man!" he groaned.

"The situation is not without its compensations. Women, mistaking your age, may bestow on you their caresses as generously as though you were a little boy. Now, may I ask—I trust you will not deem the question an impertinence—who you are and what's your little game?"

"Do you not know me?"

"Unless you are the ghost of the late lamented Peltier, I am afraid I don't."

"I am Peltier himself."

"Peltier! Ernest! Whew!" Mr. Fletcher whistled. "But I thought that you were dead."

"In the morning I shall be dead."

The little man spoke with an air of tragic gloom.

"But so far as I understand the right of the matter you are, or you ought to be, stone dead now. You are buried."

"My coffin is buried."

The little man was still. Looking at him, marking his air of extreme depression, Mr. Fletcher began, faintly, to realise the situation.

"You do not understand?"

"Not yet—exactly."

"Although you do not understand, you have ruined me. It seems to me that that is well. Is it because you love my wife?"

"Your wife! Well, not precisely."

"What is it, then? You think, no doubt, you have done a brave and clever thing—you, a stranger, who came into this country for the first time yesterday. You are mistaken. You see, I am a small man. My wife, she is as big as a house. Ever since the day I married her she made my life no life at all. I could do nothing against her; she did with me as she pleased. Once I ran away. I did not go far; I had only three francs in my pocket. Those I had to steal. Sometimes—two, three times a day—she would look to see if there was any money in my pockets. She found me, she brought me back; she locked me up for three whole weeks in this very room. She took away my clothes. She left me but my drawers, my slippers, and my shirt. That was very funny, was it not? For you, but not for me. Oh, mon Dieu! After all, I am a man."

In the uncertain light Mr. Fletcher saw that the tears were rolling down the speaker's cheeks.

"I was ashamed to complain to people of the treatment I received, though I do not doubt it was plain enough to all the world. I thought once or twice of killing her, but it seemed to me that it would be better that I should kill myself rather than her. This reflection put into my head the beginning of a scheme. At last things came to a crisis. She—she beat me. She beat me as though I were a child—me, a man of honour—with a slipper upon her knee! It is incredible, but it is none the less the truth, she beat me until I cried with pain! That was enough. I arranged my scheme. I pretended to be ill. I knew that she was very superstitious. I told her that, when I was dead, my soul would pass into the body of a horse."

"Pourquoipas?"

"Into the body of Pourquoipas. No sooner had I said it than I seemed to die."

"How did you manage that?"

"I swallowed a draught which made it seem—to her—that I was dead."

"But how about the doctor? Aren't such things as certificates of death known in this part of the world?"

"Sam Tucker saw to that."

"I thought our friend the jockey had a finger in the pie."

"He has been a good friend to me, Sam Tucker. She lost no time in putting me into a coffin. Dead, she feared me more than living. Sam Tucker fastened down the lid."

"Having first, I suppose, taken care to see that you were out of it?"

"That is so. When the coffin had been buried we got her down to the stable. I spoke to her, as she thought, out of the mouth of Pourquoipas."

"And, pray, how was that edifying performance arranged? You spoke to me, you must remember, out of the mouth of Pourquoipas."

"It was very simple. There is a cellar underneath the stable. A small grating opens into the box of Pourquoipas. I spoke through the grating. You were easily deceived."

"You think so, do you? It seems to me, my friend, that you're a past master in deception."

"My idea was to frighten my wife into sending the horses—which, after all, are my own property—and a sum of money to an address in Morlaix. Then I should be able to start the world afresh, freed from the chains of slavery. There can be no doubt she would have sent them. You came upon the scene. By meddling in the affairs of others you have ruined all. It seems that I must starve, and, after all—"

"Hist! What's that?" Mr. Fletcher caught Monsieur Peltier by the arm. "There's someone coming up the stairs, and I'll bet a dollar it's your wife. Hide behind the curtains of the bed."

There came a tapping at the door.

"Who's there?"

"Open, monsieur, open!" When the door was opened Madame Peltier stood without, in the airy costume of the night before. "Monsieur, I cannot sleep; it is no good. All the night I think that I hear voices—"

A figure advanced into the centre of the room, the figure of a very little man.

"Agnes!"

The lady fainted. Sixteen solid stone fell with a thud upon the ground. Mr. Fletcher brought her round in course of time.

"It was Ernest!"

"Upon my word," said Mr. Fletcher, "I believe it was."

"It is enough. Better to be ruined than to die. I will send the money and the horses in the morning."

And she sent them!

By Suggestion

I. The Suggestion Sent

"It is not really true?"

"Absolutely."

"Do you mean to say that when she reads that note which you are now scribbling she will at once pass into an hypnotic trance?"

"That is precisely what I mean. Her name is Carr, Jessie Carr. I shall put this note into an envelope; I shall send it round by my boy, and when she opens it and reads it she will be hypnotised. We call it hypnotism by suggestion."

"And, pray, what is the object?"

"Merely experimental. Several men will be present who are inquiring into that sort of thing. The note will be delivered in their presence; they will watch what happens, and will then proceed to test for results."

"I should like to be the young woman."

"The physical conditions which permit of such experiments are much more common, especially among women, than is generally supposed. I am going to the wedding of one of my hypnotic patients when I have sent this note."

"The deuce you are! As bridegroom?"

"Not quite. Rather an odd case. One morning a young woman came to me with raging neuralgia. She wanted to know if I could do anything for her. I said there was one possible cure—hypnotism."

"Well?"

"Well, I hypnotised her, but the cure was but temporary. She came again, and again, and again; I hypnotised her afresh each time. At last the neuralgia entirely disappeared; but during the course of the treatment I discovered that she possessed some very striking peculiarities. For one thing, she is the most sensitive subject I ever heard of."

"What's her name?"

"Her name is Miss Moore"—Mr. Wyman was addressing an envelope as he answered—"and she lives at The Laurels, in Richmond Road."

"And you say she is going to be married?"

"This morning." Mr. Wyman rose and rang the bell. A boy in buttons entered.

"Take this note at once; the address is on the envelope." The boy in buttons disappeared. Mr. Wyman turned to his friend. "Yes, Miss Moore is going to be married this morning at half-past twelve, and as it is now past eleven, if I mean to be present I haven't much time to spare."

II. The Suggestion Arrives

At The Laurels they were preparing for the wedding. Marriage is supposed to be rather an important incident in a young girl's life—it may not be so tomorrow, but it is today—and as such it involves a good deal of preparation. In an upper chamber certain persons were engaged in the sacred service of "dressing the bride." In fact, they had dressed her, but the finishing touches were needed—such touches as a painter gives to his picture on varnishing day.

"What do I look like?"

"Like a dream."

Miss Moore smiled. The comparison was not inapt. Her tall slender figure, enveloped in billows of white, was dream-like. As she looked at her reflection in the glass she felt herself that she might pass, in a picture, for a visitant from some sweet shadow land.

The young lady who had compared her to a dream spoke on.

"A dream, Bessie, that is what you look like—like some shadowy thing, which could be blown away by a puff of wind. If I were Mr. Lonsdale I should want to take you in my arms to make sure that you were flesh and blood."

Miss Moore smiled again. Other girls "said things"—such things as girls will say who minister to the wants of a bride. While they were saying them there came a knock at the door.

"A note for Miss Moore, to be delivered at once."

"For me?" She took the note in her hand. As she read the address which was upon the envelope it was noticed that an odd look came into her eyes. She seemed to tremble. Opening the envelope, she read the note which it contained. When she had done so, without a word she sat down upon the seat behind her.

"Bessie, what is the matter?" Miss Ducie came hurrying forward. It was she who had compared Miss Moore to a dream. She looked still more like a dream just then. "Aren't you well?"

She looked well—and yet she didn't.

The maid advanced—a matronly woman. She had been Miss Moore's nurse, developing, by process of natural selection, into a maid in course of time.

"Poor dear! Are you a bit faint, my dear?" Miss Moore said nothing. "She's had enough to worry her, I do think, without having something extra on her wedding-day. It's that letter what's done it. I wish I hadn't let them give it her."

"But what can be in the letter?" inquired Miss Ducie.

"I don't know. Perhaps you had better look and see."

Miss Ducie did so; but she was not an expert in handwriting, nor skilled in the deciphering of hieroglyphics, nor acquainted with the key to the cuneiform character. The contents of the sheet of paper were hidden mysteries to her. There seemed to be half a dozen lines of scribble, having neither beginning nor end.

"I don't know what it means; I don't understand it in the least. I think it must be German."

"Speak to me, my dear." The maid was bending over Miss Moore; but, apparently, Miss Moore declined to speak. "Give me the salts." They gave her the salts. Salts had no effect upon Miss Moore. "It's a queer kind of faint she's in, if it is a faint. I don't know what we shall do if we have to undress her to bring her round. It's already past the time to start."

Just then there came a loud knocking at the door. A very dictatorial voice was heard without.

"Now then, can I come in?"

Without waiting for the required permission the speaker entered. He was a tall, portly person, with something of a bully in his air. This was the bride's father, Mr. Moore.

"Do you know what time it is? It's time to start!"

As her father spoke to her, in a tone of voice which faintly resembled the discharge of an eighty-ton gun, Miss Moore turned her face in his direction. It almost seemed that the action was mechanical.

"Yes, papa."

There was something so curious in her voice that her father started.

"Aren't you well?"

"Quite well, thank you, papa."

"Then get up, and come along! Do you want to find the parson gone, and the church closed?"

In obedience to this gentle hint Miss Moore stood up. The maid interposed—

"I don't think, sir, that Miss Moore is quite well."

"Oh, you don't, don't you. You never do think that she's quite well—eh, Barnes?" Mr. Moore chuckled. He himself was in the possession of such uproarious health that the idea that anybody else could be ailing was incredible to him. His daughter's vagaries in that direction always had been mysteries. He turned to her. "I thought you said you were well?"

"So I am, papa."

Mr. Moore sniffed, made some chaste remark about "Never saw such fools as women," tucked his daughter's hand under his arm, and proceeded to lead the way to the door. But she stood still.

"Now then, move yourself! Come along, do!"

Thus commanded, she moved herself, and father and daughter led the way downstairs. Shortly afterwards the procession started for the church. The bridegroom met his bride at the church door. Mr. Lonsdale was a dapper little man, with sandy hair, which was growing beautifully less on the crown. He wore spectacles, and had an uncertain manner. His best man was John Morgan, a Welshman, who was both big and bonny.

"Bessie!"

Mr. Lonsdale advanced with hand stretched out to greet his bride; but she paid not the slightest attention to him, looking straight in front of her with a vacant stare, as though she was quite unconscious of his neighbourhood.

"Kiss the man!" exclaimed her father, in his hearty way.

As it happened Mr. Morgan also had his hand stretched out. When her father spoke, without the slightest hint of what it was she intended to do, she turned, and, with the demurest air in the world, kissed the best man on the lips.

"Good Lord!" chuckled her father, "she's kissed the wrong 'un!"

The procession entered the church. It was rather a tame affair. To begin with, the bride declined to relinquish her father's arm until he expressly bade her. Then she "hooked on" to Mr. Lonsdale's arm very much with the air of a mechanical doll. Then when the bridegroom started she, like a post, remained quite still. The result was a little chaotic.

"Step it!" said her father.

Then she stepped it. The procession went, up to the altar. The service began. Even the effect of that was marred, and that by the bride's inattention. She showed none of the ordinary signs of discomposure which commonly attend the blushing bride; but when the clergyman addressed her—as, for instance, "Wilt thou have this man to be thy wedded husband?" and so on—instead of answering she stared at him in a vacant sort of way, as though she was wondering what he was doing there. The parson was so discomposed by the way in which, without answering, she stared at him, that, taking the answer for granted, he went on with the service. Her father gave her away, and Mr. Lonsdale took her in proper form to be his wedded wife. But when her turn came to take him to be her wedded husband she stood silent as the grave.

Her father thrust a Prayer Book into her hand.

"Speak up! Read it off the book!"

She read it off the book, speaking in a curiously clear tone of voice, which could be distinctly heard all over the building.

"A man may not marry his grandmother—"

Her father had opened the Prayer Book at the wrong place. With seraphic innocence she read what was put before her. They cut her short before she got through the whole table of affinity, but after that the rest of the service fell a trifle flat. Even the bridegroom's proverbial muddle with the ring was ineffective, and that always draws a smile. When the service was over the procession was about to march to the vestry, as it seemed, without the bride. That was because the bride stood still. Mr. Lonsdale had her arm in his, but when he began to move she stood like a post.

"Bessie," he whispered under his breath; but Bessie gave no sign even that she heard. Her father came to his rescue.

"Bessie, are you deaf? Do you hear? Give us a lead!"

Then she gave them a lead. In the vestry the bridegroom saluted his bride. He might as well have saluted a statue for all the interest she seemed to take in the proceeding.

"You are nervous. But never mind, it will soon be over. Bear up," he murmured.

She did bear up surprisingly well. She was taller than he, and she stood like a lamp-post looking vacantly over his head.

People crowded round to offer their congratulations. She treated them all to the same stony inattention. Her demeanour was a model of propriety—with the chill on. They did not understand her in the least. They felt that she might at least have recognised the fact that they were there. Mr. Lonsdale bustled about explaining that the strain had been too much for her delicate organisation. He begged them to leave her alone. They left her alone. The register was signed, her signature being affixed at her father's particular request—not to say command. It seemed, indeed, that she would do nothing unless he ordered her. The thing was quite conspicuous. He drew her aside.

"Now, Bessie," he said, in that paternal way he had, "I don't want any of your foolery; no fainting fits or any nonsense of that kind. I should think you might behave decently upon your wedding-day. You just take Lonsdale's arm, and walk with him to the carriage, and go home and behave yourself until I come."

She obeyed with a docility which was more than childlike. Off went the bride and bridegroom arm in arm. The bride's father turning, saw at his elbow a short, wiry-looking gentleman, with shaven cheeks and a curiously resolute pair of eyes. This gentleman raised his hat.

"Mr. Moore, I believe? I am Mr. Wyman." The stranger handed him a card. Mr. Moore saw that on it was printed "Mr. P. H. Wyman, Surgeon-Dentist." "I don't know if you are aware of it, I think possibly not, but your daughter has been a patient of mine."

"Oh!" Mr. Moore was wondering if the stranger had chosen this peculiarly appropriate moment to advance the claims of something new in artificial teeth.

"Your daughter, Mr. Moore, has a very remarkable constitution—very remarkable" Mr. Wyman emphasised the words, looking keenly at Mr. Moore, as though to ascertain what manner of man he was. "I have been watching her in church; she seems to me to be in a remarkable condition now."

Mr. Moore waved his hand.

"My good sir, my daughter is a married woman. I've heard enough about her peculiarities all her life, and I don't intend to listen to anything more about them now. If you want to offer any medical advice you must address yourself to her husband. Mr. eh—eh—Wyman, good-day!"

Mr. Moore had driven off before Mr. Wyman was prepared with an answer to this example of parental love and native courtesy.

"She certainly seems to me to be in a queer state," Mr. Wyman told himself. "But if her father doesn't care I suppose it's no concern of mine. Nice specimen of a father he seems to be!"

III. The Ill-used Husband

The breakfast went off as flatly as the service had done. To begin with, the bride never appeared till her father went to fetch her. He had even to request her to remove her wedding-dress, it having been arranged that she was to breakfast in her travelling-gown.

"I'm sure the poor dear's not well," her maid declared, with tears in her eyes. "Bosh!" said the father. "Don't talk stuff and nonsense to me!" Then he stormed at his child. "Now, Bessie, take off those trappings, and look alive and come downstairs."

She came downstairs, if she did not look alive—and she really didn't. The meal reminded one painfully of funeral baked meats—or worse. Mr. Moore was in a towering rage, the bridegroom ill at ease, and the guests felt that they had been, and were continuing to be, snubbed and sat upon. Under such circumstances it was a relief to all parties when husband and wife were gone.

"Bessie," said Mr. Lonsdale when they were in the carriage and The Laurels were left behind, "at last we are left alone." He felt that they were alone, very much alone, when he perceived how passively she left her hand in his. "Wife! sweetest name to name a woman with! sweetest word in all the language!" He intended to be sentimental, and, in fact, tried hard to be, but when one has to try failure is predestined—especially when one's wife is sitting like a statue at one's side. "Wife, won't you speak to me?" Apparently she wouldn't. "Say 'husband' once." Not she!—not even without the h! "I really think that this is rather hard."

He really thought it was. He had heard of maiden modesty, but he felt that this was carrying the thing too far—she had been introduced to him! However, you cannot force a woman to speak any more than you can compel her to silence when she once has started conversation. So that was a silent drive. The bridegroom sat in dudgeon near one door of the brougham, the bride near the other.

When they reached the station Mr. Lonsdale, getting out, offered his hand to his wife, but she paid not the slightest attention to his offer; she sat in stony silence, with her eyes fixed on the coachman's back in front of her.

"Bessie!" he said. She paid no heed. "Bessie!" louder, but still she paid no heed. "Good heavens! are—aren't you well?"

A porter came up—a big, muscular man.

"Lady not well, sir?"

"I—I don't know," stammered Mr. Lonsdale. He didn't.

"Are you not well, madam?"

At the sound of the porter's voice she turned her head. She answered—

"Quite well, thank you."

It was a relief to hear her speak.

"But why," inquired her husband, "couldn't you speak to me?"

"Let me help you out, madam," said the porter. He helped her out.

"If you will show my wife to the train, porter," remarked Mr. Lonsdale, who felt that his position for a bridegroom—who had married for love!—was becoming a little peculiar, "I will go and get the tickets."

When he had got the tickets and a supply of literature, with which to beguile the tedium of the way, for his prophetic soul foresaw that there might be tedium, he found his wife installed in a carriage, with the porter on guard at the door. The porter, being tipped, relieved his mind to a friend.

"It's my belief that young woman's screwed, or else she's a bit wrong in the upper story. And her chap's afraid of her. A nice pair they're like to make."

The porter was wrong at least in one particular, Mr. Lonsdale was certainly not afraid of his wife. He proceeded to prove it when the train had started.

"Bessie!" No answer. "Bessie!" Still no answer. "Bessie, I insist upon your speaking to me!" He might insist, but she didn't. Seating himself on the seat in front of her, he proceeded to look at her with the most severe expression of countenance at his command.

"Bessie, do you hear what I say? I insist upon your speaking to me." Insistence being seemingly in vain, he tried remonstrance. "Have I offended you?" No reply. "Has anyone offended you?"

Silence still. She continued to look at the cushioned carriage over his head with a fixity of gaze which was positively maddening. No one would have supposed from her demeanour that she was conscious of his presence. "Look at me." But she refused even to do that. So he addressed her more in sorrow than in anger.

"Bessie, your own conscience will tell you if any conduct on my part justifies such conduct on yours. I have noticed throughout the morning that your behaviour, to say the least of it, has not been that of a bride. Heaven knows that I thought your affections were mine, but if even at the last moment you regretted your choice, why didn't you mention it?"

She didn't say. Indeed, for all the notice she appeared to take of what he said, he might have been addressing a dummy. He felt painfully the truth of this. "Very well, Bessie, I perceive my conversation is unwelcome. I will not say another word. I bought some papers, anticipating that something of this kind might happen. It is well that I did. Would you like to look at some?" He held out a handful. She did not even condescend to refuse them. "However, your way, not mine."

He went his way, which was to the other end of the carriage. There he pretended to read his paper. But his heart was sore. He felt himself ill-used. As he peeped over the top of the sheets and noted how still she sat, and the exquisite delicacy of her almost ethereal beauty, so that she seemed rather spiritual than material, he felt that this state of things was more than he could stand.

"Bessie!" he cried. "Bessie! Aren't you well? My darling, aren't you well? You know how I love you, that there is nothing in the world I would not do to make you happy. Don't look like that! If I have done wrong, forgive me, wife! wife!"

He took her two hands in his; but when he perceived how limp they were, and her utter indifference to what he said, his inability to discover the slightest clue which would unriddle her behaviour filled him with a sudden anger. He released her hands.

"Bessie, you are a wicked woman! I have heard your father call you a wicked daughter, but I never dreamed that you could be a wicked wife until today."

He returned to his papers, and there was silence. For she was no more moved by his heated words than by his protestations of affection.

This agreeable state of things continued until they stopped at a station. Someone approached the carriage, looked through the window, and then came in. He was a tall, well-built gentleman, with shaven cheeks, coal-black hair, and a pair of big, bold eyes. Mr. Lonsdale told himself that the man was an actor, or some "clowning fool"; but when he saw the stranger seat himself right in front of his wife he wished that he himself had not taken up a position at the other end of the carriage. It looked too much as though there was no connection between himself and the pretty girl in the other corner, who was so near, and yet so far away! Mr. Lonsdale wished this still more when he saw the curious, not to say impudent way in which the stranger was focussing his opposite neighbour. But there was more to follow. The man had a couple of illustrated journals in his hand.

"May I offer you a paper?" he said to the bride of the morning.

"Thank you, I should like a paper."

He gave her one! Mr. Lonsdale felt that it was time to interfere.

"I thought, my dear, you didn't care for reading."

He bustled up with a quire of papers in his hand. To his advent she paid not the slightest heed. A chill went down his back as he perceived her cold indifference. He sat by her side mumchance. The stranger stared at him with a Who-the-deuce-are-you,-sir? kind of air. Presently the fellow spoke again.

"Charming country, is it not?"

"Charming."

"Do you know it at all?"

"Not at all."

Mr. Lonsdale felt that, at all hazards, he must join in the dialogue.

"But you'll know it better soon, won't you, Bessie?"

Not a word from his wife. Not even a sign that she heard. The stranger stared at him with the Who-the-deuce-are-you,-sir? kind of air much more pronounced.

"Some nice people about here."

"Yes."

"I thought you didn't know any of them."

"No."

"Or I should have seen you."

"Yes."

"Among the nice people."

The fellow was actually paying his wife compliments before his face. Mr. Lonsdale smiled—acidly.

"My dear Bessie, perhaps this gentleman thinks that you are travelling alone."

Still not a word from his wife! The stranger gave expression to his Who-the-deuce-are-you,-sir? kind of air.

"Is this gentleman a friend of yours?"

"No."

Mr. Lonsdale could scarcely believe his ears.

"Do you know him?"

"Not at all."

Her husband gasped.

"Bessie!" he cried.

The lady did not even so much as turn her head his way. The stranger improved the occasion.

"There are a large number of queer characters who travel upon this line, principally bagmen, and such like, or worse, who make a point of entering a carriage which contains an unprotected woman, with the intention of offering her annoyance."

Although the words were addressed to the lady, the speaker's eyes were fixed on Mr. Lonsdale. Choking back his indignation, that gentleman thrust his hand into the breast pocket of his coat.

"Allow me, sir, to offer you my card."

"I don't want your card." The stranger waved it away.

"But I insist upon your taking it and my wife's card. This, sir, is my wife."

"Your wife?" The stranger seemed tickled at this. "That's pretty good." He turned to the lady. "He says you're his wife. Of course it's a lie?"

"Of course."

The stranger looked at her curiously as she said this. He seemed struck by something peculiar in her appearance.

"I don't think that you are quite well; I am afraid this fellow has been frightening you. Never mind him. You should show a bold front to this sort of person. They soon put their tails between their legs. We shall stop at another station in a minute or two, then I'll see you into another carriage."

Flesh and blood could not stand this. Mr. Lonsdale sprang up with a yell.

"Confound you! I'll wring your neck!"

"You ass! Sit down, sir! You shall have an opportunity to wring my neck when this lady has gone. Then I shall have a word or two to say to you on my own account."

Mr. Lonsdale wiped his brow. He took off his glasses and wiped them too.

"Bessie!" he cried; "Bessie, speak to me! Are you mad?" In his distress and perplexity he even descended to an explanation with the stranger. "Sir, this lady is my wife. We were married not two hours ago; we are on our honeymoon, and since we left the church door she has not—spoken to me—a single word!"

Mr. Lonsdale actually broke into sobs. The stranger significantly nodded his head.

"I suppose the man's a lunatic."

"I suppose he is," said the "lunatic's" wife.

"Never mind! This is the station. I will see you into another carriage here."

The train was drawing up at the platform. Mr. Lonsdale caught his wife by the arm. "Bessie! What are you going to do?"

"How dare you! you impudent scoundrel!" Mr. Lonsdale suddenly found himself hurled with considerable violence to the other end of the carriage. "Porter!" Putting his head through the window, the stranger summoned a porter. "This man has been annoying this lady. Just look after him while I see her into another carriage."

"She's my wife!" screamed Mr. Lonsdale.

The guard of the train came up.

"Do you know this person, madam?" He alluded to her husband. The lady said never a word. The stranger came to her aid.

"He has nearly frightened her out of her senses. I should judge, from his behaviour, that the man's a lunatic. A sane person would scarcely behave in the way he has done." He spoke to the lady: "The man's a perfect stranger to you, is he not?"

"A perfect stranger."

"She's my wife!" screamed Mr. Lonsdale. "I swear she is."

"Come, that won't do," said the guard. "I saw the lady get into the carriage by herself, and you only got in just before the train was starting."

This comes of allowing a porter to escort your wife to a carriage! The consequences were, that just when Mr. Moore, at The Laurels, congratulating himself on having got rid of a troublesome daughter, was thinking of departing westwards to dine, there came a fatal telegram. He tore it open with a grin.

"I suppose they've wired to say that they have arrived safely at their journey's end, or some tomfoolery or other. As though I cared!"

The message which the yellow envelope contained was this:—

"Come down at once. My wife has gone off with another man.—William Lonsdale."

Of this telegram Mr. Moore could not make head or tail. It was dated from a little roadside station some sixty or seventy miles along the line.

"I suppose it's a joke. A pretty sort of joke! 'Comedown at once.' Yes, I think that's very likely. Without my dinner. I daresay. 'My wife has gone off with another man.' What, Bessie? No doubt! Why, there isn't enough of the devil in her to do such a thing. And on her honeymoon! She's done some funny things, has that young woman, but that would be the funniest of all. I'll catch myself going down at once if she's gone off with fifty men. I'll send a wire to see who this telegram has come from, then I'll have something fit for a Christian to eat. It will be the first decent meal I've had since the girl was born."

In the meantime, something a little singular had happened to Mr. Wyman. He was going along the street—quite a natural action, be it observed—when he encountered an acquaintance. No less a person than Dr. Pilbeam. Pilbeam's obstreperous scepticism on the subject of the recent developments in the direction of hypnotism has made him quite a topic of the day. Mr. Wyman stopped him with a smile. "Well, Pilbeam, are you satisfied?"

"Quite."

"I thought you would be."

"I thought I should be too."

There was something in Pilbeam's manner which the other did not understand, even a dryness which he did not relish.

"I thought you would have waited till I came myself to remove the suggestion."

"To remove what?"

"The suggestion."

"Hardly necessary, was it? since the suggestion never came!"

Mr. Wyman started.

"Pilbeam! What do you mean? You don't mean to say that when Miss Carr read my note she did not at once pass into a state of hypnotic trance? I can scarcely credit it. There must have been some blunder."

"I don't know, Mr. Wyman, if you have been having a little joke at our expense."

"A joke! Pilbeam!"

"I can only say that I, in company with half a dozen men, have been kicking our heels for the best part of the day in the house of a young woman of the name of Carr, waiting to see the latest wonder—hypnotism by suggestion, but somehow the suggestion never came."

"But I sent the note!"

"Did you? In that case you had better inquire where it went to. It never came to us."

Dr. Pilbeam nodded his head, and walked away, more sceptical than ever! Mr. Wyman tore home at a pace which the seven-leagued boots never could have equalled. Arrived there, he rang a peal, which brought the boy in buttons on the scene as though he had discharged an electric gun.

"You young rascal! Why didn't you deliver that note I gave you?"

"I did, sir."

"You young liar!" Mr. Wyman actually clutched the wretched buttons by the throat. "What have you done with it?"

"Please, sir, I took it, sir, to the address, sir, what was on the envelope, sir. Miss Moore, The Laurels, Richmond Road, sir."

"What!"

Mr. Wyman started back. He was aghast, as well he might be!.

"Please, sir, it was wrote upon the envelope!"

"What was on the envelope?"

"Miss Moore, sir, The Laurels, sir, Richmond Road, sir."

"Are you quite sure?"

"Please, sir, quite, sir! And I took it, sir! And I told the young woman, sir, what opened the door, sir, to give it to the lady at once, sir. I'm sure I did!"

The boy began to blubber, his master's manner was really such a strange one.

"And she gave it her! That explains it!" This remark was addressed to vacancy, and not to the boy. "You—you can go!" This was to the boy. "No, stay! No, you can do no good you've made enough mess of it already—get outside!"

Buttons went outside. Mr. Wyman was left alone to face the situation.

"That explains it! Good heavens, what an ass I've been! All those fellows waiting at Miss Carr's, and I sent the suggestion to Miss Moore! It was all through that confounded Turner. We were talking about the thing, and I was telling him about Miss Moore, and I must have addressed the envelope to her without noticing what it was that I was doing. Such things do happen, but they never happened to me before, and I'll take care they never do again. But—!" He sank into a chair as though struck by a sudden shock. "By George, I believe it acted! The suggestion took effect upon Miss Moore! Great Caesar!" He started up with a very curious look upon his face. "I'll stake my life it did! Her behaviour in the church— at the wedding—I couldn't make it out! She was married in a state of hypnotic trance!" Mr. Wyman stood in the centre of the room in a state of semi-stupor. "The thing is inconceivable, but, by Jove, I do believe it's true! But—!" The whole beauty of the situation came rushing on him all at once. "But, if she was married in a state of hypnotic trance, then—she's in it still! Great Great Jupiter! What—what shall I do? It it strikes me that I had better go and see."

Mr. Moore was just going down the steps at The Laurels when a cab tore up, and a man sprang out of it as though he were springing for his life.

"Mr. Moore! Thank heaven!"

Mr. Moore stared at the newcomer, gradually recognising in him the "Surgeon-Dentist" who had spoken to him outside the church in the morning.

"Well, sir, 'Thank heaven!' I shall thank heaven if you will allow me, sir, to go and dine."

"But, Mr. Moore—your daughter!"

"Confound my daughter! And I should like to know what interest you take in my daughter's movements, Mr.—Mr.—What's-Your-Name?"

"Is she inside?"

"Inside? Not if I know it! She's got a home of her own to go to, thank the Lord!"

"But—where is she?"

"What on earth, sir, has that to do with you? You're a stranger to me!"

"But this is a serious matter, Mr. Moore. Will you allow me to say a word inside?"

"Oh, come along! come along! I'm starving; I haven't had a meal for days, but of course that's not of the slightest consequence to anyone, and least of all to me." As he was speaking Mr. Moore led the way into the house. "That girl's been a trouble to me ever since the day she was born. I've always said she would drive me into my grave, and so she will. It's not ten minutes since I had a telegram—"

"A telegram! You've had a telegram?"

"Do you know about it then?"

"I! How should I? But if, as I suspect, it concerns your daughter, if you will acquaint me with its contents, I think, Mr. Moore, that it will expedite an explanation."

"Oh, if it will do that I shall be delighted! An expeditious explanation is just what I am waiting for. Besides, it's a sort of telegram which a father would be proud to show to any man."

Mr. Moore handed Mr. Wyman the message. Mr. Wyman read it aloud.

"'Come down at once. My wife has gone off with another man.' It's just what I expected."

"Just what you expected! Hang it, this is charming! Do you mean that you took it for granted that a daughter of mine would show her husband a clean pair of heels on her wedding-day? A nice sort of family you must think we are!"

"Mr. Moore, do you remember my speaking to you outside the church door with reference to your daughter? Did you not yourself notice something peculiar in her manner?"

"If it comes to that, I never noticed anything about her that wasn't peculiar. I tell you again and again what I tell everybody, that that girl has been the plague of my life ever since the day she was born."

"Did your daughter receive a note this morning?"

"How on earth am I to know? Do you suppose that I spy on her correspondence?"

"Perhaps you would inquire."

Mr. Moore went into the hall and shouted up the stairs—

"Barnes! Barnes!"

Barnes appeared.

"Did Bessie have a note this morning?"

"Yes, sir; I've got it in my pocket now. She left it behind."

"Then bring it in here."

Barnes entered the room, and handed the note to Mr. Moore.

"And when the poor dear looked at it she seemed to go off quite queer."

"She did, did she? Why couldn't you tell me that before? But you can expect nothing but deceit from a pack of servants! Perhaps you can make something of this; I can't."

Mr. Moore passed the note to Mr. Wyman. Recognising his own hieroglyphics he addressed himself to Barnes.

"You say that when the young lady received this note—what happened?"

"Well, sir, she went off into a sort of faint—she seemed quite strange."

"And then?"

"Well, sir, she didn't pay any more attention to what I said than if she was dead. The only person she took any notice of was her pa."

"That will do. You can go."

Barnes went.

Mr. Wyman turned to Mr. Moore.

"I am sorry to have to tell you, Mr. Moore, that your daughter was married in a state of hypnotic trance."

"In a what?"

"In a state of hypnotic trance. But perhaps you will allow me to explain?"

"I should be glad if somebody would—before I go stark mad!"

"I am a dentist, Mr. Moore. Some time ago your daughter came to me half beside herself with neuralgia."

"She has suffered from it ever since she was a child—that among other things. I believe she has suffered from every mortal malady—or she says she has."

"So she informed me. I told her that under those circumstances a remedy would be hard to find, but one I did suggest—hypnotism."

"Hypnotism! Isn't that the new-fangled word for mesmerism?"

"Precisely. I told her it might effect a cure. At her own urgent request—remember, Mr. Moore, she was half beside herself with pain, and talked about suicide, and all sorts of things—I hypnotised her there and then."

"The devil you did!"

"The neuralgia disappeared, but its disappearance was only temporary. It returned, and on its return she came again."

"She never said a word to me about all this."

"I daresay not. I hypnotised her again and again, the neuralgia recurring each time less acutely than before, until finally it disappeared entirely. And this is where the curious part of the tale comes in."

"Well, I don't know!—I should have thought that the curious part had come already!"

"It has been discovered quite recently that it is possible, in certain cases, to induce the hypnotic trance by what is called suggestion. The operator, by writing a few words upon a sheet of paper, and taking care that that sheet is delivered to the subject, can at once throw, even while he is himself at a distance, the subject into a state of trance."

"Good heavens!"

"The existence of this power has been doubted, and to prove that it actually does exist I had arranged that this morning a series of illustrative experiments should take place in the presence of a certain number of medical men. The subject chosen was a young lady of the name of Carr. As I was penning the note which was to convey the suggestion I was talking over the whole matter with a friend. Incidentally I mentioned the case of Miss Moore. I suppose that it was owing to that that in a fit of absence of mind I wrote her name and address upon the envelope. Anyhow, I did so, and in consequence the suggestion was conveyed to her."

"Well, I'm—well, I'm!" Apparently adjectives failed Mr. Moore, for he got no further. "And is that the note of suggestion which you hold in your hand?"

"It is."

"And do you mean to say that my daughter was mesmerised by the mere sight of it?"

"I do."

"But I thought that people when they were mesmerised became insensible. She seemed sensible enough to me."

"As a rule a hypnotic subject can be influenced by the operator only, but your daughter's is a peculiar case; she is super-sensitive. I think it possible that she might be influenced by anybody in whom the hypnotic power was either latent or developed. I have no doubt that it is latent in you."

"In me!"

"In you. From what the servant has said, with reference to your daughter only taking notice of her father, I have no doubt that it exists in you. It is more common than people are as yet aware. Indeed, you may say broadly that all strong-minded and strong-bodied people possess hypnotic power more or less."

"It seems to me that I am learning something even if I am destined to starve, and it appears I am!"

"On the other hand, to people in whom that power did not exist, even in the germ, she would, to all intents and purposes, be dead; to her, so to speak, they would be simple negations. For instance, perhaps it does not exist in the gentleman whom she has married."

"In Lonsdale? I shouldn't think that he had any power of any kind."

"In that case he has found her unmanageable, and she has fallen under the influence of someone who, to judge from the telegram, has used her for purposes of his own. We must go down at once, as the sender of the telegram requests."

"What! Without my dinner! Don't I tell you that I haven't had a meal for weeks!"

"You can eat something as we go. Or I can go without you. Expedition is of vital importance. I don't wish to unnecessarily alarm you, but the misadventure which has begun with something like a farce may result in something like a tragedy."

Mr. Moore groaned and went. As the travellers reached their destination, and the train began to slow, Mr. Moore put his head out of the carriage window. As he did so, he gave an exclamation suggestive of surprise.

"Hollo! There she is!"

Mr. Wyman sprang to his side.

"Who? Your daughter?"

"My daughter! And Lonsdale too!" Mr. Moore returned into the carriage. "Is this a joke of yours? Is it a confounded hoax? Is all that stuff you have been telling me a pack of lies? If it is—"

Mr. Moore did not say what would happen if it were, but his inflamed countenance meant volumes. In silence Mr. Wyman took up the position his companion had just quitted—that is, he put his head out of the window. On the opposite platform of the station a nice little scene was being acted. A tall, slender, and exceedingly pretty girl was locked in the embrace of a short, plump, spectacled young man, and they were saluting each other with a total disregard of anything in the way of false shame, which is not generally recognised as a common feature of English manners as they are to be seen in public. By their side stood a tall, dark gentleman, who was observing their proceedings with what seemed to be a smile of approbation. Mr. Wyman, as he beheld these things, could scarcely believe his eyes.

"It—it is your daughter, and—and she seems quite well."

"Seems quite well! She is quite well! I'll be even with some of you for this!"

And the enraged father leaped out of the train and hastened to the opposite platform with an agility which did credit both to his years and size. His appearance on the scene produced another little tableau. The young lady, releasing the young gentleman, ran towards him with a cry.

"Papa!" she cried. "Papa!"

But the fond parent repulsed her with an air of violence which must have been a shock to her feelings, and to the feelings of the lookers-on—of whom, by the way, there was quite a gathering.

"Now don't give me any of your nonsense! You've made sufficient exhibition of yourself, without making an exhibition of me."

Mr. Moore turned on his daughter's husband with a roar. "What do you mean by sending me that telegram, you—you—you—"

Once more Mr. Moore was at a loss for "language." The bridegroom, mopping his brow with his handkerchief, poured forth a flood of eloquence with which to appease his father-in-law.

"I have gone through a series of experiences today which, if they hadn't happened to me, I should never have thought could have happened. My wife ran away with another man—"

"Oh, William, don't say that!" And the bride smiled a beautiful smile to the bridegroom of an hour.

"Well, I won't, but—but—but I don't know what I shall say if I don't. I—don't understand it yet, but it appears that if it hadn't been for the gentleman she ran away with—"

"William!"

"I was only going to say that so far as I understand at present, if it hadn't been for him I might never have seen you again—never! never!"

Mr. Wyman's interposition cut short the harassed bridegroom's confession of bewilderment.

"I think I have an inkling of the riddle." He turned to the tall, dark gentleman who still stood beaming in a benevolent kind of way. "I think you and I have met before."

"You are Mr. Wyman," said the stranger.

"And you are Mr. Christopher. You assisted in the experiments in hypnotism which recently took place in the hospital of La Salpetriere in Paris. I was struck with some of the results which you produced."

"You are very kind. I remember to have had the pleasure of seeing you there."

IV. The Penitent Wife

They dined at the Station Hotel. When Mr. Moore's appetite was somewhat appeased, Mr. Christopher made a personal explanation.

"I have played a somewhat ambiguous part today—I have run away with another man's wife. I must ask the lady's pardon, and I think it will be allowed that it is only right that I should ask the gentleman's too.

May I do so in all due form? But this I would say, that no sooner had the elopement begun"—here there was a twinkle in the speaker's eyes—"than I perceived that there was something wrong. When I found myself alone in the carriage with the lady, it dawned upon me more and more that in her manner there was something very strange. All at once it came upon me, like a flash of lightning, that she was in a hypnotic trance. I cannot tell you how startled I was by the discovery. I do not know that I need be ashamed to own that for a moment it took away my presence of mind. How did she come into such a state? Was it possible for me to remove the influence of another? I tried, and—well, I succeeded. She became her own proper self again. She cried, 'Where am I? Who are you?' I answered all her questions as I could, but I trust—and I know that my pious aspiration will be echoed by more than one!—that I may never find myself in so equivocal a situation again. At the next station we alighted. There being no train due which would enable us to retrace our steps for some little time, I telegraphed to the injured husband a confession that I had, unconsciously, been guilty of a crime."

"I shall never forget my feelings," exclaimed the blushing bride—for she now was blushing—"when I found myself, in a railway carriage, alone with a—a stranger."

"And I never shall forget mine," observed the bridegroom, "when I received that telegram. They had locked me in the waiting-room, and set a man on guard to see that I didn't do myself a mischief. But when that wire came, I took the change out of them, I can tell you."

"And to think," cried the lady, "that I should have been married, and known nothing about it all the time." She turned to Mr. Wyman, "I do think it was a little hard."

"It was a little hard," he owned.

It was!

A Silent Witness

I. The Living Death

I doubt if a more terrible thing ever happened to any man than that which happened to me in the autumn of 1883. The memory of it all is with me now as though it were but yesterday. And sometimes I wake shrieking in my dreams, and lie awake all night, oppressed with a great agony of fear. I was a clerk in Burton's Bank at Exeter. For some days I had been queer and out of sorts. More than once I had been conscious of what seemed to me a sudden numbness of the limbs. For instance, on two separate occasions I had been incapable of rising from my office-stool. My wife and fellow-clerks noticed that I did not seem to be in my usual health, and my wife in particular had been urgent in entreating me to take my annual holiday without delay. But I had some complicated accounts to balance which I was unwilling to leave undone. And that more especially since they had given me an infinitude of trouble, the sought-for balance being exactly the thing I could not get.

It was the evening of September 14th. It was a Friday. I had decided at the last moment to remain at the bank after the rest had gone, for I had arranged that if I could get the accounts all right I would start for Penzance on the following morning with my wife. God alone knows how I yearned for a sight of the sea!

It had been a hot day, that Friday—a terribly hot day—and all day long I had been conscious not only of a curious unwillingness, but of an absolute incapacity, to move. In some extraordinary way my limbs seemed in a measure to have passed from my control. I suppose it was past six o'clock. I was all alone in the bank; the rest of the establishment had left a good hour ago. I was leaning forward on my desk, racking my brains to think where the error could be, when—shall I ever forget it?—in an instant—in a flash of lightning—I became conscious of a singular sensation which was stealing over me. It was just as though some malevolent spirit had woven a spell and deprived me of the power of motion. I was spell-bound, rooted to my seat, as helpless as though I had been struck by the hand of death.

The strangest part of it was that while in that sudden, awful visitation I had lost the use of my limbs, I had preserved my faculties intact. I could see—straight in front, that is—for not only could I not turn my head a hair's-breadth to either side, not only could I not even close my eyes, but I could not even change the direction of my glance. I could only look straight in front of me with what I felt instinctively must be a fixed, horrible, glassy stare. But what there was in front of me, that I could plainly see. And I could hear. Indeed, my hearing seemed to be unnaturally keen. For instance, Burton's Bank is in the Cathedral Yard. Not only could I hear every footstep which passed even on the other side of the Cathedral—no slight distance for the sound of a foot to travel—but I could hear the traffic that went up and down Fore Street Hill, and over the bridge, right away to St. Thomas' on the other side. And worse—for God knows that in the horror of all that followed it was of a surety the worst of all!—I could think. My brain, like my hearing, seemed to have become phenomenally clear. Instantaneously I knew what had come upon me. It was catalepsy. I was in a cataleptic fit!

I felt no pain—physical pain, at least. In that sense I was like a man whose physical side is dead, but whose mind still lives. And as I sat there hour after hour, dead, my agony of mind rose to such a climax that I cannot but think that it transcended whatever agony of body the most morbid imagination has at any time described.

It became dark—so dark that my eyes became useless for any purposes of sight, and yet they would not shut. It became silent, too—the intense silence of the night. But all at once, when the night was stillest, a sound struck on my ears—a peculiar sound, as of someone who walked with muffled steps. And then—could it be? Yes! A window was being opened close at hand.

I cannot doubt but that the only thing which had kept me from promptly falling on to the floor when the fit had first taken me, was the fact that I was leaning so forward that the greater part of my weight was on the desk. So, leaning forward on the desk, I stayed. Just in front of me was a glass partition, on the other side of which was the inner office, in which the safe was kept. It was the window of this inner office which was being opened now. By what I cannot but suppose was a providential accident, since I could not alter the direction of my glance, the safe was right in my line of sight; and so, although I could not immediately see who it was that entered, directly the mysterious intruder came between myself and the safe I could see him plainly.

At first all was dark. Then a light was struck, and someone, bearing a shaded lantern in his hand, appeared in my line of sight.

It was Philip Morris, our head cashier, and practically the manager of the bank!

I shall never forget my unutterable amazement when I perceived that it was he. What could bring him there at such an hour, in such a way? He wore a light dust coat which was unbuttoned down the front, so that I could see his dress-clothes beneath and the diamonds gleaming in his shirt.

He carried a small leather bag in his hand. He took a bunch of keys from his pocket; with these he unlocked the safe. From it he took a quantity of notes—I could hear them rustle—and several bags of gold, which jingled as he dropped them in his bag.

Then he turned right round, so that I saw him full in the face.

"If Wheeler could only see me now!"—I should mention that my name is Wheeler—Richard Wheeler. The allusion was to me. "I guess he would soon unriddle the mystery of his accounts. Well, the game is up, I suppose; I have had my fling, even if the result is penal servitude for life. I flatter myself that few men would have had the dexterity to carry it on so long."

He came a few steps forward, the lantern in his hand, and suddenly stopped short. His eyes were fixed on the glass partition. On his face there was an expression of the most awful ghastly fear. His lips seemed parched; he gasped for breath. For a moment I thought he would be seized with a convulsion, but he had sufficient control over himself to ward off that. He spoke at last, and his voice was like the voice of a strangled man.

"Wheeler! Wheeler! Is it you? For God's sake, don't look like that! Your eyes are horrible!"

He covered his own eyes with his hand; I could see him shudder. Then he looked again; his mood was changed. With quick, firm steps he advanced to the partition door, and entered the office in which I was.

"I suppose you think you have caught me?" he cried. "I congratulate you upon your cleverness; but perhaps, my friend, you have caught more than you think."

Suddenly he seemed struck by my immobility. He came a step nearer.

"Why do you sit there like a wooden block, you hypocritical old fool? Do you hear? Can't you speak? You think you have trapped me very neatly, eh?"

He paused, he came a step nearer.

"Can't you speak, you fool? Wheeler! Wheeler!"

He laid his hand upon my shoulder; he shone the lantern in my face. Suddenly he gave the most dreadful shriek that ever yet I heard.

"My God!" he cried, "he's dead!"

In his sudden fear the lantern fell from his hand with a crash. He gave me a push which sent me flying head-foremost to the floor. And where I fell, there, like a dead man, I lay.

II. The Conscious Corpse

I lay on my own bed in my own room. Oh! what had I ever done to deserve the agony which I endured then? There was my wife on her knees beside the bed; there was a candle which flickered on the chest of drawers, although daylight already streamed into the room; and there was I, wrapped in the garments which enfold the dead. How my wife wept! How she mourned in the sudden anguish of her woe! Now she called on God for mercy and for strength, and now she got upon the bed and pillowed her head upon my breast, or bedewed my face with her kisses and her tears.

"Richard!" she cried. "Richard! After all these years! My own! My dear!"

And then she wept as though her heart would break. Who shall conceive my agony as I lay there?

A little later there was this scene. Five men came into the room. There was Dr. Leverson, my old medical attendant; Wilfrid Burton, the banker, whom, man and boy, I had served for thirty years; Mr. Fellowes, the lawyer to the bank; Philip Morris, that accursed thief; and Captain Philipson, the chief of the county police.

It was Mr. Burton who spoke first. His voice was dry and cold—very different to the kindly, pleasant voice I knew so well.

"Before we go any further, I suppose, Dr. Leverson, there is no doubt that this wretched man is dead? That you certify? No autopsy necessary, or anything of that sort?"

Dr. Leverson smiled a superior smile.

"Richard Wheeler is certainly dead. I have the certificate of death in my pocket. The funeral is already arranged. He died from valvular disease of the heart—a disease of whose presence I have long been aware." My brain reeled as I listened to the glib announcement. "Doubtless his death was accelerated at the last by a sudden shock."

"God," said Mr. Burton, with a solemnity the unconscious irony of which was hideous, "saw fit to strike down the criminal at the moment of his crime."

I wondered what Philip Morris looked like as he heard the words. This time he was out of my line of sight.

"And now," continued Mr. Burton, "to proceed to the business which has brought us here. I need not point out to you, Dr. Leverson, that all that passes here is in the strictest confidence." I presume that the doctor bowed his head. "The bank has been the victim of—"—the speaker's voice trembled, and I felt that my wife covered her face with her hands—"of the most terrible dishonesty. To what extent the affair has gone I have not yet had time to ascertain, but I fear that we have been robbed to the extent of at least a hundred thousand pounds."

A hundred thousand pounds! My God! No wonder I could not get the accounts to balance! That villain had robbed us of a hundred thousand pounds at least, and I lay speechless there.

"Mr. Morris will repeat the statement which he has already made to me. You, Mr. Fellowes, will kindly take it down, and we will have it attested in the presence of Captain Philipson. Mrs. Wheeler, you need not stop; it will only be painful to your feelings. Indeed, I think you had better go away."

"Sir," said my dear wife—oh, how her dear voice rang through my brain!—"whatever Mr. Morris may have to say, I never shall believe that my dear husband was a thief. I have known him to be a true husband and a God-fearing man for nearly thirty years."

"Ah, Mrs. Wheeler, how appearances may deceive. I had to the full as much confidence in him as you. Before you think that I misjudge him, hear what Mr. Morris has to say."

Philip Morris began his tale. It flashed upon me in an instant that he had availed himself of my supposed decease to fasten his guilt upon my head. But I had never imagined that anyone in his circumstances could have carried the matter through with so easy an air. There was even an affectation of pathos in his tones as he filled in the details of his horrid lie.

"I had been spending the evening at Mr. Fisher's"—Mr. Fisher was one of the minor canons, a bachelor, who was reputed to have a taste for whist and for hours which were, perhaps, a little uncanonical. "I was returning home, when, on passing the bank, I noticed that there seemed to be a light in the office in which the safe is kept. The window, as you know, is but a few feet from the ground. I have often pointed out how easy it would be for a thief to get in that way."

"I know you have! I know you have!" said Mr. Burton.

The hypocrite went on:—

"To my surprise I found it was unlatched. I opened it. Whoever was within was too much absorbed in his occupation to notice what I did. I looked through the open window and saw that someone was in the inner office, but who it was I could not at first perceive. I climbed through the window and went in. Directly I entered the man looked up; it was Richard Wheeler. When he saw me he gave the most awful scream I think I ever heard, and fell down—dead. So soon as I had recovered from my bewilderment, I went to the window and called for help. A constable who heard me came to my assistance. Together we examined the room. That is all I have to say. I only wish that I had not to say so much."

"But there is more that must be said," Mr. Burton took up the strain. "In the grate were found the half-consumed fragments of the accounts, which, if they had been suffered to continue in existence, would inevitably have betrayed the dead man's crime. The safe was found wide open—it is still a mystery how he contrived to open it—ransacked of all the chief valuables it contained. On his desk was found a bag containing five hundred pounds in gold, and in his pockets notes for a thousand pounds. But notes and gold to the value of ten thousand pounds, and securities to a very large amount, are gone. We have still to find out where. I am sorry to tell you, Mrs. Wheeler, that to search this house is one of the purposes which has brought us here."

"Sir," said my dear wife, "you need make no apology. You are welcome to search the house from attic to basement. You will find nothing that was not righteously my dear husband's own."

III. The Coffin Breaks

For five days I lay there—dead. Words cannot describe the agony I endured. Conceive it if you can. Picture yourself in my position; conceive what you would suffer then. Far better had I indeed been dead.

On the second day they came and measured me for my coffin. Think of it—a living man! On the fourth day they brought it home, and I was placed within. There were two of them that brought it, and as they placed me in that narrow box they cracked their little jest.

"A tight fit, isn't he?" said one.

"Ah," replied his fellow, "they'd have given him as tight a fit if he had lived; four good strong walls for life."

"Who'd ever have thought old Dick Wheeler would have done a bit upon the cross?"

"Well," again replied his fellow—how I loathed that man!—"I would for one. I never knew a psalm-singer yet that wasn't a robber and a thief."

When that choice pair had gone, my wife came in and looked at me as I lay in my last bed. She had a wreath in her hand, which she placed upon my breast, and a white rose, which betokened innocence, which she placed within the wreath. She stooped and kissed me on the brow; and as she did so she burst into a flood of tears.

"Oh, God!" she cried, "show that my dear husband was not a thief!"

The next day, the fifth, they came and screwed me down. Imagine that! I learnt from what they said that they feared that if, in that hot weather, I was left for a longer time exposed, decomposition would set in. When they had already placed the lid upon my coffin, my wife came running in. I learnt that they had come in her absence to shut me for ever from her sight. They imagined that if she were there she might object to what they did. Her appearance disconcerted them. She made them immediately remove the lid, and bade them withdraw from the room, so that she might have final solitary communion with her dead.

She knelt down by the side of my coffin and prayed. She expressed the most profound belief in the innocence of the man who had been her husband for nearly thirty years, and she besought the Most High that He would expound that innocence, and make it clear to man. Then she stood up and kissed me on the lips—kissed me a last good-bye!

Then she left me, to the full as broken-hearted as she herself, and the undertaker's men returned and screwed me down. They put the lid upon my coffin, and shut from me the blessed light; for no one had closed my eyes. They had tried to, but the lids would not come down. I could hear the traffickers in death laughing and jesting as they drove the screws well home. When they had done their work, and gone, I was a prisoner indeed.

How long I remained in that box screwed down I never knew. It seemed to me a hundred years. A dreadful thought came to me, not once but again and again, with recurring force. Suppose that I indeed was dead? Who knows the mysteries of death? Is it not conceivable that when the body dies, the mind, which has such a mysterious affinity with the soul, may live? If I were dead, and my shame should live! Was it possible that through the long cycle of the years, the aeons, which were still to come, my mind should be alive and I be dead? . . . It is not strange that my pen should tremble as I recall the thoughts which racked me then.

Racked me with such intensity that, even in my state of death, I feared I should go mad. And then? What then? Mad through the aeons in the womb of time! Even dead, I thought my brain would burst. I tried to scream. I struggled as with the issues of life and death for the power to give expression to the great agony of my fear and pain.

And then? What happened then? To this hour I cannot precisely say. I know that while, mentally, I struggled with inconceivable eagerness to cry out, I suddenly awoke. I know no other word to use. I knew I was alive. Alive, and prisoned in that box! And I do believe that for the first few moments of my resurrection—what was it else?—I actually was mad. I had a madman's strength, at any rate. I struggled like a madman, too—struggled to be free—and with such strength that I burst the box, forced the coffin's sides, and was a prisoner no more.

I stood upon my feet. As I did so I discovered that my display of strength must have been a sort of frenzy, for indeed I was so weak that at first I could not stand. I sank back upon the bed. But only for a moment. There was that within me which gave me strength. I was filled with an overmastering desire to proclaim my innocence and bring home to the criminal his crime. Wholly regardless of the clothes I wore, forgetful of them even, I went down the stairs into the street, and ran to Mr. Burton's as certainly I never ran before.

I must have cut a pretty figure as I ran, but Mr. Burton's great house was within a couple of hundred yards of my more modest residence, the hour was late, and I never met a creature on the way. I was well acquainted both with the banker's habits and his house. I knew that often, when the rest of his household was fast asleep, Mr. Burton would sit for hours writing in the study which opened on to the lawn at the back. To this room I hastened. It was as I supposed. There was a bright light within. I turned the handle of the French window; it yielded to my touch. Without pausing for an instant to reflect on what the consequences of my act might be, I burst into the room.

As I entered, Mr. Burton was sitting writing at a table. He looked up. When he saw me he rose from his seat. He clutched the edge of the table. He gazed at me, speechless, unable to believe that what he saw was real.

"Wheeler!" he gasped at last; "Richard Wheeler!"

"Yes, sir, 'tis I! Not dead, but living! This is no ghost you gaze upon, but a creature of flesh and blood, to whom God has given strength to declare his innocence and expose another's crime."

I poured out my tale. He was too bewildered at first to grasp the meaning of my words. It was all so unexpected and so strange that he was unable to realise that he was not the victim of some dreadful dream. But it became plain to him at last. It was painful to see his agitation as he began to grasp the purport of my revelation.

"You had a cataleptic fit!"

"If it was not catalepsy, I know not what it was. I am no doctor, sir."

"And you were within an ace of being buried alive! The thought is terrible."

"It was terrible to me."

"And you saw—you actually saw—Philip Morris rob the safe?"

"I was a silent witness of his crime. It was only when he supposed that I was dead that it occurred to him to place the guilt upon my shoulders."

"What a villain the man must be! It seems incredible! But the whole story seems incredible for the matter of that, and the most incredible part of it is your presence here. But even supposing what you say is true—and God forbid, after what you have told me, that I should deny it—how are you going to prove his villainy?"

"Mr. Burton, I am but newly come from the chambers of death."

"For heaven's sake don't talk like that! You make my blood run cold."

"But the fact is so; and things are revealed to me which to you are hidden." I rose up, still in my grave-clothes, trembling like a leaf. "At this instant the thief is at his work again, and tampers with the safe. Mr. Burton, I entreat you to come with me to the bank; his villainy shall be proved to-night."

"Come with you—to the bank—at this hour of the night!"

But I had my way. The banker lent me some of his own clothes, and a cloak was thrown over my shoulders. The coachman was roused; a carriage was ordered out. Within a very few minutes we were seated in it, and were being driven swiftly towards the bank, through the silent streets, to catch the criminal in the very moment of his crime.

The carriage was drawn up some little distance from the bank. We got out. Mr. Burton had the key of the private door. We approached swiftly, yet silently as well. Our chief object was not to give the slightest alarm.

On the very threshold Mr. Burton paused.

"I am afraid that this is a wild-goose chase that you have brought me on. Some folks would even call it by a stronger name."

"Can you not hear him? Hark! He rustles a bundle of notes! They are those notes which were missing, and which you searched my house to find."

"Hear him, Wheeler? Are you mad? When he is in the private office—if he is anywhere at all—and we are out in the street!"

"I can hear him, if you can't. Give me the key, or open the door. Every moment which we waste increases his chances of escape."

Hesitatingly—I believe he doubted my sanity even then—Mr. Burton put the key into the lock. Noiselessly it turned. Without a sound the door swung open on its well-oiled hinges. We stood inside. It was pitch dark.

"Hadn't we better have a light? I cannot see my hand before my face. We shall be falling over something if we don't take care."

"I need no light. Remember my eyes have grown accustomed to the dark. You, sir, have only to keep close to me."

I led the way. He followed close upon my heels. Suddenly I paused.

"See! There is a light!"

Sure enough there was, in the inner room—in that inner room in which the safe was kept. I caught Mr. Burton by the arm. "Sir, come a little farther, and you shall see it all. You shall see the criminal detected in his crime."

I did not tremble then; I had become quite cool and calm.

I knew my hour was at hand. With unfaltering fingers I unloosed the cloak from about my shoulders and stood revealed in my cerements, as though I had new-risen from the grave. And then—

Then I stole by the outer door into the office in which I had been overtaken by that strange mockery of death. Through the glass partition, sure enough, I saw at a glance that Philip Morris, lantern in hand, was at his old work, busied with the contents of the safe. I leaned right forward on the desk, and tapped with my fingers against the glass. He caught the sound at once, but for a moment did not perceive from whence it rose. He approached the partition; I saw him trembling as he came. I saw his face was ghastly white.

When he was quite close, in my grave-clothes I rose straight up, and, looking him straight in the face—his pallid, panic-stricken face—I raised my arm above my head, and in a loud voice cried out—

"Thou thief!"

A wild shriek rang through the night; and sometimes in my ears I seem to hear it still!

When Mr. Burton and I ran in we found him, stricken by a sudden agony of conscience-stricken fear, a bundle of bank notes in the frenzied grip of his right hand, lying in a fit upon the floor.

To Be Used Against Him

I. A Travelling Companion

When the train left Liverpool Street, he and I were the only occupants of the compartment. I was in one corner, he was directly opposite me in the other. He appeared to have purchased the same evening papers which I had purchased. I noticed, too, a certain similarity in his movements to mine. When I lowered my paper he lowered his. When I turned a page he turned one also. This coincidence of action I supposed, at first, was accidental. But I perceived, ere long, that, if it was accidental, the accident was of a peculiar kind. Whatever I did he did. When I exchanged one journal for another, he exchanged one also. I noticed, in this respect, that the imitation was so close, that when I relinquished the Pall Mall for the St. James's, he relinquished the Pall Mall for the St. James's. When I put my paper down and looked at him, he put his paper down and looked at me. I asked myself if this person intended to insult me. What conceivable reason could he have for entering a railway carriage with the apparently deliberate intention of insulting an inoffensive stranger? Unless he was drunk, or mad?

Directly I began to observe him I was struck by the fact that he resembled someone whom I had seen before. Who it was I could not, for the instant, recollect. I eyed him—while he eyed me—endeavouring to recall to my mind who was the owner of his features.

"I believe that I have had the pleasure of meeting you before."

When I addressed to him this commonplace, which so frequently is addressed to individuals whose personality one fails to recollect, to my surprise he replied to me in exactly the same words which I had used—

"I believe that I have had the pleasure of meeting you before."

The tones of his voice were familiar to me. I had not only heard them before, but I had heard them recently.

"You are laughing at me because I cannot recollect your face? And yet it is proverbial among my friends that I have an excellent memory for faces."

Scarcely had I finished speaking than he echoed me. He repeated, after me, word for word what I had said. The man must be a mountebank. And yet, the longer I looked at him, the better I seemed to know his face. Who was the fellow?

"May I venture to ask your name?"

The only reply which I received to my inquiry was my inquiry echoed. The man must be some clowning spirit, who, in revenge, perhaps for my bad memory, proposed to amuse himself a little at my expense.

"When you are pleased to be more communicative, I will endeavour to apologise for my imperfect recollection."

"When you are pleased to be more communicative, I will endeavour to apologise," came the echo from the opposite corner.

I confess that I was conscious of a certain feeling of irritation. The mildest of men does not care to be mocked, and I am not prepared to say that I am the mildest of men. Still I did not propose to have, in a railway carriage, any unpleasantness with a man who, after all, might be a perfect stranger to me. So I gathered my papers and my wraps together, and withdrew to the other end of the carriage. Scarcely had I done so when the man who had been in front of me did likewise. He gathered his papers and his wraps. He came and planted himself in front of me at this end, as he had done at that.

There could be no doubt that the action was intended to be impertinent. The thing was done too deliberately to admit of any other supposition. Still I was not prepared to show resentment. I did not see how I could do so, that is, with any regard to my own dignity. I could scarcely have a vulgar squabble with the fellow then and there. The boat train does not stop between London and Harwich. We were compulsory companions while the journey lasted, unless I threw him out of the carriage window or he threw me. Better to endure his insolence, unless it became aggressive, until we reached our destination.

I became tired of reading. I put down my paper, the man in front of me, in pursuance of his apparent policy of faithful imitation, simultaneously put down his. He returned the look with which I favoured him. But to that I was indifferent. I continued intently to study his countenance, asking myself when, and where, before our meeting in that carriage, I had encountered him before.

He looked a gentleman; I was prepared to admit that he was a gentleman. He had about him that indefinable something which the trained observer inevitably associates with his idea of a gentleman. He was probably between thirty and forty years of age. He was good-looking, with a long, sallow, oval face, which was innocent of moustache and whiskers, and a very curious mouth and chin. I think it was the peculiarity of that mouth and chin which impressed one with the consciousness that he might not be an agreeable man to quarrel with. There was something about the formation of the lower part of his face which was suggestive—though only to my imagination, perhaps—of cool, calculating, unflinching cruelty. I say that this might have been a suggestion of my imagination, but his eyes conveyed not merely a suggestion, but an absolute certainty. They were the most beautiful eyes which I had ever seen. They were large and black—jet black and deep, so deep that it seemed impossible to penetrate their depths. The pupils had a curious trick of dilation like a cat's. They were large at first, and seemed to gleam with light; as you observed them they grew perceptibly smaller, until but a point remained—a point of light. No man could look at that man's eyes and doubt that he was as cruel as the grave.

The unflinching way in which he met my gaze had a curious effect upon my nerves, though I am far from being a nervous man. The more I continued to observe him the more persuaded I became that we had met before—not once, but constantly—so firmly were his features impressed upon some mislaid tablet of my memory. Yet, try how I would, I could neither remember where I had seen him nor who he was. This was the more extraordinary, because he was possessed of so distinct an individuality that one was disposed to say that one need only set eyes upon him once never to forget him.

I could restrain my curiosity no longer. I leaned forward and, regarding him fixedly, I said—

"Don't I know you?"

He leaned forward and, regarding me fixedly, replied—

"Don't I know you?"

It was but an echo; the man persisted in his mockery. And yet the tones of his voice—with what a strange familiarity they seemed to ring in my ears, and, at the same time, how they grated on my nerves, how they filled me with a sense of irritation. He had advanced his face to within a few inches of my own. In the irritation of the moment I was more than half-disposed to strike him; the palm of my hand itched to salute his ears. I believe that I should have struck him had I not, all at once, become conscious of the look which was in his eyes. The pupils grew and grew until they glared at me more like a wild beast than like a man. I drew back in my seat, stifling an exclamation. There could be no doubt whatever that murder was in the man's eyes—that he was mad.

I lost him when we reached Harwich. I went at once to the Antwerp boat. The night was glorious. I remained on deck while the boat was being cast from her moorings, after she was out in the river, after she was out in the sea. I had no desire for a cabin; I did not trouble myself even to secure a berth; I had no desire for slumber. I, of course, was conscious that, in my peculiar circumstances, sleep was a factor not to be neglected. Without a proper amount of sleep a man's nervous system is bound to suffer, and when his nervous system suffers the man suffers altogether; he loses perfect control of his mental faculties. To keep perfect control of my mental faculties was, to one in my position, literally a question of life or death. It is, I firmly believe, only when a man loses perfect control of his mental faculties that the police score what they call their successes.

Therefore, to me, a proper amount of sleep was indispensable, but at the same time I was aware of what was the exact amount I did require, and I knew that I wanted none just then. I was in no mood for slumber; I was in a mood to enjoy the perfect night, the fresh breezes, and the smell of the sea. And I was in a mood, after a while, to think—of Alan Foster. I wondered if he was still lying where I left him, with his face to the ceiling.

I am quite willing to admit that I felt a certain satisfaction in picturing him to my mind's eye exactly as I left him. I felt a certain pleasure in painting as vivid a picture as my imagination would allow me of the room in which I left him; a picture of the little details of the room—his chair and mine, the shaded lamp upon the table, the look upon his face when, in that last, swift moment, he understood that I meant— business, the inanimate thud with which he had banged on the floor. I wondered if he had made much mess, whether I ought to picture him with or without the adjuncts of a crimson pool. If I had possessed the secrets of the magicians I would have travelled back for an instant just to see. I had frequently speculated as to what would be the sensations of a man in my position. I do not know that there was anything remarkable about my own. I should say, in no extraordinary sense, that my sensations were those of satisfaction.

When I had had enough of thinking of my last meeting with Alan Foster my thoughts recurred to the fellow in the train. As I leaned over the side of the steamer I taxed my brain with an effort to recollect where I had seen him. Again and again I had almost hit upon his trail, when it again escaped me. I could not think who the man might be. I wondered if he was in the boat, bound with us for Antwerp, or whether he was journeying in the boat to Rotterdam. Thus wondering, I stood up, and turning to the smoke-room, which was just behind me, saw him at my side.

I own that I was startled. I had supposed that I was the only person upon deck. He certainly had not been there a moment back. I had heard no one approach, yet there he was, leaning, as I was leaning, with one hand upon the side of the vessel, his eyes fixed intently upon mine.

For some moments we continued, in silence, to observe each other. As we did so I was conscious that his glance began to fill me with a species of vague discomfort—if I may say so, with a sort of horror. It was absurd to suppose that I should allow him to continue to amuse himself at my expense. I spoke to him.

"May I ask, sir, if you have any intention of dogging my steps?"

He said nothing. He continued to look at me. And the more he looked at me the less I liked the look of him.

"Is it not a fact, sir, that you and I have met before?"

"It is."

The voice in which he uttered the two little monosyllables was such a familiar voice, a voice which was so well known to me, that the mere fact of its exceeding familiarity filled me—although it may appear exaggeration on my part to say so—with a vague sense of pain. Surely the sound of that voice had been ringing in my ears for years!

"May I ask, sir, where we have met before?"

He was silent. Less and less did I like the expression which was in his beautiful eyes.

"May I ask, sir, what is your name?"

"I have no connection with the police."

It is true that the peculiarity of his demeanour, the intentness of his gaze, the sense of discomfort with which I was conscious that his presence began to fill me, had led me inwardly to inquire if the fellow could be in any way connected with the police. But I had not formulated the inquiry in words. How came he, then, to reply to my unspoken query? Could he be connected with the hounds of Scotland Yard? The suspicion of such a possibility filled me with a sudden passion—with one of those ugly rages for which, among my friends, I believe, I am well known. I moved towards him, bent on mischief. As I moved towards him he moved towards me. His eyes were fixed on mine. I protest that of no man living have I ever been afraid, and of no man dead; of things of flesh, nor of things of air. I have never hesitated, even for an instant, to do anything because I was afraid—witness my career! I protest that, until that moment, I believed myself to be incapable of the thing called fear. But when, in that moment, I met his eyes, and saw them well, and, in the moon-light, clearly—I was afraid. I slunk away, and stole into the smoke-room, and left him there.

When I entered the smoke-room, still tingling with the consciousness of having played the coward, I found it in the possession of three persons. Two were upon one seat, and had arranged themselves in such a position that each was able to stretch out his feet on the seat in front of him. Both were asleep. The other seat was occupied by a single individual. He, also, was asleep. He lay stretched out at full length upon the seat in such a manner that, at his feet, there was only left space enough to enable me to crowd myself in the corner. This vacant space I occupied. As I sat there, in that cramped position, my feelings towards that luxurious individual were not of the friendliest kind. He was evidently in the enjoyment of perfect comfort—he was actually snoring!—while he had left me scarcely room enough to breathe. I was telling myself that it would serve him well right if I were to pull his nose with sufficient vigour to rouse him out of his state of selfish stupor to a consciousness of the requirements of the situation, when the door opened, and the man came in from whom I had slunk away. He paid no attention to me whatever. He stood looking down at the snoring sleeper. As he looked the expression of his countenance was simply diabolical; it startled even me as I sat looking on. Lower and lower, towards the sleeper, he bent his cruel, handsome face. Suddenly, putting out his hand, he grasped the sleeper's nose, and wrung it with such savage ferocity that I half expected to see the nose torn right off the victim's face.

No man could continue wrapped in slumber whose nose had been handled in such fashion as that man's nose was handled then. The snorer not only ceased to snore, but he sprang to his feet and emitted a yell which must have been audible throughout the ship. The little apartment was in confusion. We were all of us upon our feet. The sufferer fondled his nose—as well he might! The adjectives which proceeded from his lips my pen is unable to record.

"Who did it?" he yelled. "Who did it?"

He glared at each of us in turn, as if disposed, in the first paroxysms of his pain, to regard us all there as guilty parties. His actual assailant had vanished, like a coward, through the door. I was just about to point this out when, to my amazement, the man who had been sleeping just in front of me charged me with the assault. I repelled the charge with all the indignation with which, on the impulse of the moment, I was capable. The man declared that he had seen me do the deed.

"Why," I cried, wholly at a loss to conceive what could have induced him even to imagine such a thing, "you were asleep."

"I was between sleeping and waking," he replied. "I saw you looking at that gentleman; I saw you lean over him, and I saw you pull his nose."

If I had not shown the sufferer pretty clearly that discretion upon his part would be the better part of valour, I believe that he would have attacked me there and then. I declared, upon my honour, not only that my accuser lied, but that I was incapable of the conduct with which he charged me. I explained whose was the guilt.

"The man came in, and looked at you, and pulled your nose. Before—so completely was I taken by surprise at what seemed to me to be so unprovoked an outrage—I could stop him, he was gone again."

We went out to look for the miscreant. We sought for him in all directions. But he was not on deck. No signs of him were to be seen. We asked the watch if he had noticed anybody moving. He declared that he had noticed me, but that, with the exception of myself, no one had been on deck for the last hour or more. It is certain that the sailor was deceived—as he might very easily be in that uncertain light—but the gentleman whose nose had suffered looked at me, as though if he only dared he would.

I know not if the story got about, and if the general verdict was that I was the guilty party, but it certainly seemed to me, throughout the rest of the journey, that the whole of the passengers gave me plenty of elbow-room. Not a soul could I get to exchange a word with me during our passage up the Scheldt. Whoever I spoke to immediately found that something required his presence in another portion of the ship. More than once, before we arrived at Antwerp, I was on the point of showing my resentment. But, until we drew up at the quay, I never caught even a glimpse of the ruffian for whose outrageous conduct it seemed I was temporarily suffering.

I entered the train for Brussels. It seemed, until just as the train was starting, that I was to have the compartment to myself. When the signal had been actually given, and the train was already in motion, the door at the opposite end of the carriage opened, and the man came in who had wrung the unconscious sleeper's nose half off his face. With the calmest air in the world he came down the carriage, and placed himself on the seat in front of me. This was a little more than I could stand.

"As you have come in, sir, you must excuse me if I get out."

I put my hand through the window to unfasten the door, but the engine had got up steam. We were clear of the station. To have attempted to alight would have been to infringe the by-laws of the railway company. I should have found myself in the hands of the authorities. There was nothing for it but to make the best of the situation, and to treat my unwelcome companion with all the philosophy at my command. I put my legs upon the seat; I prepared to take my ease. My companion did exactly as I did; he put his legs upon the seat, and he prepared to take his ease. But I was not to be moved by such a trifle as that. If it was his humour to play the mountebank, his humour caused no sort of inconvenience to me. As the train moved through the flat country which lies between Antwerp and Malines, and beyond, I, for my part, was wrapped in thought, until the silence was disturbed by my companion.

"It's not bad fun, this running away from the police."

The fellow's words so exactly interpreted the thoughts which had been passing through my brain, that I could not help but let him see that I was startled. I moved my legs from off the seat, and turned and faced him. Still bent on imitation, he turned himself towards me. The fellow filled me with such a sense of curious repugnance that I was at a loss for words with which to address him. He, however, seemed to be completely at his ease. He began, leisurely, to remove his gloves. Having removed them, he held out towards me his hands. I noticed what white, slender, artist's hands they were.

"Look at them! They're white enough, they're without a stain. And yet they're dyed in blood!"

He spoke in the tone of voice which seemed to be so intensely familiar.

"They're dyed with the blood of a friend—of the best friend man ever had. I killed him, my best friend."

He leaned back in his seat. There was a smile about his lips which seemed to me to be the incarnation of all cruelty.

"I killed him because I hated him; and, a little, I think, because he loved me so. He had always trusted me, and I had always played him false, and the more I played him false the more he trusted me. For that I hated him. I robbed him of his moneys, and he pretended that the things which I had stolen had been his gifts to me. For that I hated him the more. So, having robbed him of great things all his life, I robbed him, out of pure pastime, of a little thing—I robbed him of his wife. This fool, he loved his wife; he loved her, I do believe, better than his soul. So, when he learned what I had done, just for the sport of it, he dared to show resentment, for which I killed him, there and then. I killed him when his heart was hot with rage against his well-tried friend. That was yesterday, at six. I left him there, just where he fell, upon the floor. I went round to my rooms. I slipped a few things in my dressing-bag. I caught the boat-train at Liverpool Street. I'm en route for Brussels, and after that I know not where."

The fellow laughed softly to himself—it was the most dreadful sound I had ever heard. Was he man, or was he devil, that he could read the inmost secrets of my heart, only to make a jest of them like that? It was not his own tale he had told, it was mine. I had slain my friend only a couple of hours before I had met this fellow in the Harwich train. Already, I did not doubt, the avengers of blood flattered themselves that they were upon my heels. How came this man to know what was hidden from all the world but me? I knew not what to say to him—what was there to be said? Unless I took him by the throat, and crushed the life from him. I would have done it had I dared. But, for the second time in my life, my courage failed me—I did not dare. There was something about this man which I knew so well—it frightened me. I racked my tortured brain with the unanswered, and it seemed unanswerable question—where had I seen this man before?

Not another word was spoken upon either side until we reached Brussels. As the train drew into the station I arose, and said—

"Well, is it your intention to accompany me further?"

He shrugged his shoulders, and he smiled. I went out, and I left him sitting there. But all the time, as the cab drove through the busy streets to the hotel, I felt as though that man were sitting in the cab there at my side.

II. The Haunted Man

After dinner, by way of a little relaxation, I went to a certain café where there are women who sing. I do not pretend that the place was a place of particularly good repute, or that the entertainment which it offered was in any sense worth listening to. As a matter of fact, the performance was execrably bad and abominably dull. Indeed, the place was a vulgar and blackguard place, and therefore excellently suited to the humour I was in, for I was in a black-guard frame of mind. I sat drinking the poisonous concoction which they call "absinthe d l'anisette," while one of the chanteuses, a hideous fat woman, hovered about me and asked for drink. On the table next to mine there were some papers. I drew them towards me. Among them was a London paper of that day's date. It was uncut. It had travelled quicker than I had, having probably reached Brussels by the Ostend route. Opening it, my eyes searched down the columns. They lighted on a paragraph which was headed, "Dreadful Tragedy in Sackville Street." I read the paragraph. It was a narrative, up to date, of Alan Foster's murder.

It seemed that they must have discovered the body only a few minutes after I left the house. Alan's man had gone to the room and knocked, and having received no answer had tried the handle, and found that the door was locked. He waited some minutes, then returned, and, as he still received no answer to his knocking, fearing that Alan was ill inside the room, he sent for assistance, and had the door forced open. Braithwaite had been in the service of Alan's father. He had tended Alan himself almost since he was a child. I pictured the old man's face as he saw his master lying dead—murdered—on the floor. It seemed that the body had made a mess. The newspaper said that the corpse was discovered lying in a great pool of blood. I could not altogether understand how that could be. I was positive that I had spitted the heart with one blow, given with Alan's own stiletto, a long, slender weapon, scarcely broader than a bodkin. It seemed hardly probable that much blood would flow from such a wound as that. The paragraph concluded by stating that the police were on the track of the assassin, and that a warrant had been issued at Scotland Yard. So! we shall see.

When I had finished reading this instructive item of current news, a chanteuse came round, a scallop-shell in her hand, soliciting subscriptions to compensate her, in some measure, for the vocal agony which she had been recently enduring. As I glanced up, to drop some sous into her shell, my eyes chanced upon a man who was seated at a table right in front of me, but on the opposite side of the room. It was the man of the train! He, too, was reading a journal, just as I had been doing, and apparently his was an English journal too. As I looked at him he looked at me, and, raising the paper, pointed to a particular paragraph it contained, indulging in that soft, devilish laughter of his, which seemed to fill my very soul with horror as I heard.

The sensations with which I regarded this man, and heard his horrid laughter, and felt his eyes upon my face, filled me with a feeling of the profoundest physical repulsion.

"My God!" I cried unconsciously aloud. "Who is this man?"

The chanteuse still lingered in front of me. She supposed that my question was addressed to her.

"Which man? That man sitting at the table there! Mon Dieu! Is it not monsieur's Corsican Brother?"

The woman's words struck the chord which had been vibrating in my memory, yet which had escaped my keenest search. No wonder I supposed that I had seen this fellow's face before it was so like my own. And as the sudden revelation of the fact that this was so flashed upon my brain, such a sense of horror came rushing, whirling over me, that I staggered like a drunken man. The woman must have thought that I was mad, because, so soon as I had recovered sufficient self-control, I rushed out of the place, and into the busy street beyond.

I tore along the Boulevard du Nord like a thing possessed. Such was my haste, that I came into unwitting contact with someone who was advancing in the contrary direction to my own. It was a little child a little girl. Such had been the force of the collision that I had flung her back upon the stones. I picked her up; I took her in my arms; I soothed her tears. She was a little thing, thin and pale, and poorly clad. I made her distress my own. I pressed some silver coins into her hand, and begged her to forgive my unintentional transgression. The sight of the silver coins seemed to have more effect even than my words in the drying of her tears. She looked at them, and through the tumult of her grief there already dawned a smile. I was just about to make my peace and leave her, happy in the possession of her new-found wealth, when a man came striding across the street at the rate of a good six miles an hour. It was the man whom that chanteuse had suggested was my Corsican Brother. He caught the child from off the ground; he struck her with his hand; he kicked her with his foot; he tossed her out into the gutter. It was the cruellest thing! And then, as she lay crying where she had fallen, he turned to me and pointed to her, and, laughing, disappeared into the crowd, leaving me standing where he had come on me, riveted to the ground.

The child's cries attracted the attention of the passers-by. They advanced to her assistance; I advanced with the rest. But, to my amazement, the ungrateful creature cried out the more at the sight of me, and shrank back as though I were a plague. "What is the matter with you, little one?" inquired the bystanders.

"He beat me; he kicked me; he threw me out into the road."

The little child stretched out her hand towards me, as though I had been guilty of these things. The wickedness of such a charge, made by one whom I had so recently befriended, for the moment took my breath away. But instead of treating the child's wanton accusation with the incredulity which I naturally expected, the bystanders turned on me with black looks and lowering brows. "To treat a little child like that!" they said.

"Messieurs et mesdames!" I exclaimed; "so far from treating a child like that, I would not injure a single hair upon her head. This little child is labouring under some extraordinary delusion; it was not I who did this thing. The miscreant who was guilty of this wanton cruelty vanished as quickly as he came. He was a stranger, ladies and gentlemen, to me; but rather than this little child should suffer, even at a stranger's hands, I will present her with a napoleon with which to dry her tears."

"It is not money which will pay for conduct such as that."

The people crowded round me. There were some of them whose fists were clenched. The looks with which they regarded me were anything but looks of love. Ominous murmurs were in the air. It would have needed but little to have induced them to lay on me hands of violence. It was with the greatest difficulty that I appeased their anger. It cost me five napoleons to dry the sufferer's tears.

Such incidents as that, if repeated, were likely to prove expensive, to speak of nothing else. It was with feelings of the strongest resentment towards the scoundrel who hung upon my footsteps that I pursued my way towards my hotel. More than once I suspected that he was at my side, or just behind me. Once I distinctly heard his footsteps keeping pace with mine. I turned. He was peering over my shoulder, actually pushing his face against mine.

"Well?" he said, and smiled.

In my sudden, justifiable fury I struck at him. He nimbly moved aside, so that he escaped my blow. Laughing that low, soft laugh of his, before I could pursue him he vanished in the crowd.

It was certain, if I was to continue to endure the infliction of this fellow's presence, that my health would suffer; and chiefly on my health rested my chances of safety. If it failed me, it was not impossible that I might fall into the toils of those bunglers at Scotland Yard. They would then say, "You say that we never make a capture; see what a capture we've made now!" when all the time it was not their wit which had prevailed, but it was that fiend who hung upon my heels who had played into their hands. I resolved to go straight to bed.

When I reached the hotel I noticed that the man from whom I demanded the key of my apartment seemed to look at me askance.

"I am tired," I explained. "I have been travelling all night. I am going to get some sleep; it is that which I require—sleep."

The man said nothing; but it seemed to me that he was extremely careful to keep himself at arm's length of me. What was there about my personal appearance which should make this fellow anxious not to come in contact with my person, or which should cause him to stare at me like that? As I ascended the staircase I met a young woman who was coming down—servant of the hotel, or some such thing as that. She had a smile upon her face, but when she caught sight of me, and her eyes met mine, the smile vanished. I never before saw so sudden and so singular a change come over a woman's face. She shrank away from me sideways, against the wall, as though she was afraid that I would strike her.

"My child," I said, "what is the matter with you? You stare at me as though I were a ghost."

She did not answer me, and she ran down the stairs with the swiftness of the wind. What should induce the woman to behave like that? If there was anything curious about my face, it was owing to the want of sleep. It was only sleep which I required—nothing more.

"At last," I cried, when I entered my apartment, "at last I am alone, free from all that noisy crowd, in the enjoyment of my own company. Now for slumber—for a little closing of my eyes in sleep."

As I moved across the room I remembered that I had omitted to lock the door. It would never do to overlook that ceremony, or that ill-omened wretch, in his measureless impertinence, might even venture to invade the precincts of my bedchamber. I turned to supply the omission, and, in the very act of turning, perceived that the man had been before me. I was too late.

The fellow had taken instantaneous advantage of my slight forgetfulness, and already had forced himself upon my privacy. He stood only a step or two in front of me, with a look upon his face such as surely is only to be seen upon the faces of the fiends in hell. It was a look which I had not seen before. It was instinct with some dreadful meaning. The pupils of his eyes were distended to a monstrous size. They gleamed as if with fire.

But I was not to be frightened by his threatening looks at a moment such as that. I had come there to seek that peace which seemed to have eluded me since yesternight. And if I could not have peace I would at least have privacy. I would not have my solitude polluted by the presence of that thing of evil. He should go out—he should go out, even though in the struggle there was murder done, and he murdered me, as I had murdered Alan Foster, in his room, the night before. With my blood coursing through my veins, as if it were a stream of liquid fire, I advanced upon that messenger from hell. As I advanced on him he advanced on me. I stretched out my arms to take him by the throat, he copying my actions in all their details. I gave a spring to grasp at him, the wildest passion burning in my heart, and—I struck against a mirror!

I struck against a mirror—Oh, my God!

The thing of evil which I thought to grasp was but the image of myself, mirrored in a glass. That creature, on whose countenance was pictured all the passions of all the fiends, was my own image, mirrored in a glass. That human animal, whose eyes gleamed cruelty, and shouted murder, was my own image mirrored in a glass. The dreadful being who had been my almost constant companion since the moment in which I had struck the devil's blow, and who had read the inmost secrets of my heart, and whose ostentatious wickedness had so filled my soul with loathing, had been, all the time, but the image of myself, mirrored in a glass!

I could not believe that the thing could be. I could not believe that the messenger from hell was formed in my own likeness. But it was so—there could be no doubt about it—the thing was as plain as day! A mirror ran from floor to ceiling. I stood close up to it. There, staring at me in the silvered glass, a smiling fiend, was—myself!

In that dreadful moment, when I first realised what manner of man indeed I was, my legs trembled beneath me, and I would have sunk upon my knees to plead for mercy from my God, only that I lacked the courage. It was not for me, whose hands ran blood, to speak with God. And yet it would have been better that I had dared. For as I stood there, striving to obtain the courage which should enable me to shape my lips in the utterance of a prayer, there came a touch upon my shoulder, and turning I beheld at my side the man in the train. He pointed to the mirror, and he smiled—as he always seemed to smile—a devil's smile.

"You see we make a pair. I am you, and you are me. How strange you should not have known me when first we met. How strange you should not have known your own voice when first you heard it, echoing, in the train."

I knew it now—I knew my own voice as it proceeded from his lips. Then I understood how it was that its exceeding familiarity had seemed to fill me with such a sense of bitter pain.

"I have been sent in order that you may be able to see just what sort of man you are. I am the power which has been given you to enable you to see yourself as others see you. I will be with you to the end—a mirror ever ready to your hand."

He stopped, and he whispered in my ear; and he smiled—a devil's smile.

"You know, it was murder. There was nothing gallant in the deed. It was the act of a coward and a cur. See, it was like this!"

He took me by the arm, and he turned me round. And I saw a table, on which there was a shaded lamp. And at this table sat a man, and his face was that of a true man, and the light in his eyes was pure and good. And I knew that it was Alan. And this fellow went and sat on a chair which was on the other side of the table, and he looked at Alan. And as the lamplight fell upon his features I noticed what a difference there was between his looks and Alan's. They both were handsome men. But Alan was a fair-haired, blue-eyed, open-faced, English gentleman. The other's was the cleverer face; but there was something in it, notably in the expression of the mouth and of the eyes, which repelled; something which told me, as I stood watching there, that the heart within the man was evil. And Alan said—how well I knew his full, clear voice!—and as he spoke there was a cloud upon his sunny face—

"Jack, I hope you won't mind my saying what I'm going to say, but I was bound to ask you here so that we might have it out between us; I was bound, old man."

The man upon the other side of the table smiled.

"My dear Alan, pray don't apologise."

"Jack!" Alan rose. He began pacing to and fro. He seemed to have that to say which he found it difficult to utter. "Jack, you remember when Doris left me, how—how—how my heart was broken. You are quite sure, Jack—I only ask it as a matter of form, old man, because, of course, I know that no man ever had a better friend than you have been to me—you are quite sure, Jack, that you knew nothing of her going?"

The other was a moment or two before he answered. And during that moment or two he smiled. There was, lying on the table, a long, glittering, slender blade, which Alan had brought home with him from

India, and which it had been his habit to use as a paper-knife. The blade was so slender, the temper of the steel was so true, and the handle was so heavy, that one had but to hold it, point downwards, five or six feet from the ground, and drop it, for it to bury itself almost to the hilt in the wood. The man on the other side of the table drew this odd paper-knife of Alan's to him. He began to play with it. As he did so his smile became a very peculiar one indeed.

"My dear Alan, don't you think it is unnecessary for two such old friends as you and I to pay any attention to mere matters of form? Besides, it is nearly two years since Doris left you. Some men would have forgotten such a wife in a week. I thought she was forgotten long ago."

"Forgotten! You thought that I had forgotten Doris, Jack! Forgotten her—my darling! I shall never forget Doris while I have life. If she were to come back to me this moment, or if she comes back to me in ten years' time, I will take her to my arms again—if she will only come; and I will forgive her everything. But you have heard me say that sort of thing over and over again. Just answer me my question, Jack. You are quite sure that you knew nothing of her going?"

"My dear Alan, don't you think that it is rather late in the day to ask me such a question as that?"

"Of course I know it's late in the day, and of course I know that the whole thing's an absurdity. But the fact is, old man, some men—some men have been saying—"

Alan paused, as if he were at a loss for words. The man on the other side of the table continued to smile and to trifle with the paper-knife.

"Well? Some men have been saying—what?"

"Some men have been saying that you knew more about her going than you pretended; there's the truth for you, old man."

There was a slight pause. When the man upon the other side of the table spoke there was something so peculiar in his tone of voice that even blundering, slow-witted Alan must have noticed it.

"My dear Alan, it would be just as well that you and I should have a clear and perfect understanding, once for all. It will have to come one day, and why not now? I wish you clearly to understand that I am as sick of hearing Doris's name as I am sick of Doris."

"Jack!"

"Alan!"

"What do you mean?"

"I say that I am as sick of hearing Doris's name as I am sick of Doris. That is what I say, and that is what I mean."

"You are sick of Doris? Do you—know where she is?"

"I know very well indeed where she is."

"Jack! Where is she?"

"She's in a house for which I pay the rent; but, thank goodness, with your money and not with mine. It is only right, my dear Alan, that you should pay house-rent for your own wife."

"Jack! say—say that you lie!"

"My dear Alan, I shall not say that I lie, because I don't." It seemed that Alan could only gasp. "Doris ran away with me, you fool! She never cared for you a pinch of snuff from the beginning. When I acted as your best man, and she stood by your side at the altar, I knew that it was for me she cared. It was the old story of 'Il y a toujours un qui aime, et l'autre qui permet'; always, Alan. When you had married her, I thought I would take her from you. So I took her. It was the easiest thing. The joke of it was, that you never suspected it was I. You made of me your confidant instead; and what a blind fool you've always been, dear boy! But the thing has got beyond a joke. Doris has become a nuisance. I never cared for her! As I said, I am as sick of hearing Doris's name as I am sick of Doris."

There was a pause. Alan said nothing; but with the cry of a wounded lion he rushed upon the man who sat on the other side of the table. The man waited for his spring. Just as Alan was upon him, he rose, holding the glittering weapon with which he had been playing above him in the air. He drove it to the hilt into Alan's breast. Without the utterance of a sound Alan banged backwards on to the floor. I saw him lying there, and I knew that he was dead. My dearest friend! He whose chief crime had been that he loved not wisely, but too well.

The wretch who had done this deed of darkness turned towards me, and said—with, about his lips and in his eyes, that devil's smile—

"You see—it was like that you did it!"

I covered my face with my hands, and tried to hide from my eyes that dreadful sight. And when again I removed my hands, the table with the shaded lamp had vanished, and the dead man upon the floor, and there was nothing there but that wretch, who regarded me with his unceasing smile.

And as I looked at him and he at me, the door of the apartment opened, and three men came in, one of whom advanced to the wretch standing in the centre of the room. He laid his hand upon his shoulder, and he said in cold, stern tones—

"John Alton, you are my prisoner. I arrest you for Wilful Murder."

There was a flash of something in the air. I knew that a pair of handcuffs had been produced. The wretch had remained quiescent for a moment, as if stupefied by an unexpected blow. But when he saw the glittering fetters he leapt upon the officer, and, in an instant, he bore him to the ground. The others ran to the assistance of their fallen comrade, or there would have been another murder done, and I should have seen a second corpse lying on the floor before my eyes. The guilty wretch, in his wild frenzy, bit, and scratched, and tore, and kicked, and fought, and screamed, and yelled, like the thing which indeed he was—a fiend from hell. Strangers streamed into the apartment. The room was filled with people, and in their midst the one man against the three. They fought like devils here, there, and everywhere. But at last they mastered him the three against the one and in that same instant the scoundrel vanished.

And I lay there upon the floor, torn, and scratched, and bruised, and bleeding, with gyves upon my wrists. And they dared to say it was I who had struggled. They lied! Why should I have struggled? Was it because I was afraid of them? Does it look as though I were afraid of them, now that I am writing this, every word of which they tell me will be used against me? What do I care what they use against me? I repeat it once more, in black and white, it was I killed Alan Foster—I! And it is my complete conviction that, under the same circumstances, I should kill the fool again. The so-called "terrors of the law" have no terrors for me. They are quite welcome to take me to any place of execution they may please, and there to hang me by the neck till I am dead.

The Words of a Little Child

I. The Mother and Daughter

A dirty room, with, in it, a ricketty table, a wooden chair without a back, an empty sugar box, used as a stool, and in a corner on the floor a heterogeneous collection of odds and ends, which served as a bed. Very little else, except a woman, a little girl, a black bottle, and a cup without a handle. To the woman the black bottle was far and away the most prominent object in the room. All that, in her judgment, was needed to adequately furnish a room was a bottle of gin. And there was still the better part of a pint of gin in that black bottle. She was making it last as long as she could.

The woman sat on the chair without a back, and the little girl on the empty sugar box in front of her. And the woman took sips from the cup without a handle, and she groaned: "Your father's a wicked man; he's a devil."

"Yes," said the child. She spoke in a shrill, clear treble. She was only seven, though her form was wizened, and her whole being was saturated with sin. "He's a devil."

"No one knows what your poor mother has had to bear from that father of yours."

"He's always a-beating of you."

"It's gawd's truth, my lovey."

"An' now he's a-going to kill yer."

"That he is."

"But I'll 'ang 'im for it, mother."

"That's a good girl to the mother what loves yer." The woman wiped her bleary eyes with a corner of her filthy rag of an apron. She took another sip from the cup; she looked at the child with the cunning grin of the woman who has lived for years practically on nothing but gin. "You've been a good daughter to your poor mother, and I've been a good mother to you, haven't I, Louisa?"

"A better mother never was!"

Suddenly the woman looked over the child's head. She pointed with quavering finger towards a corner of the room; she trembled with excitement.

"There's another of them, Louisa, there's another! A great black thing, with long 'air and a bushy tail, I see it drop from the ceiling. Look alive, girl, move yourself; don't let it get at me!"

The girl moved herself. Going to the spot indicated she went through the pantomime of stamping on, and kicking at, nothing at all. In a child of such tender years the gravity with which she did it was, in its way, sublime.

"That's all right, mother, I done for it."

Her mother began to cry.

"Whatever I should have done without you, Louisa, I don't know. You've been a blessing to your poor mother. Take another sup, my girl, only don't you take too much, 'cause there's only a little left in the bottle, and it's the last drop of comfort your poor mother'll have in this world."

And the woman wept profusely. The child took a sip from the contents of the cup. When she had drunk she mimicked the action of a cat—she put out her tongue and she licked her lips.

"Mind you 'ang your father, girl!" Mrs. Drewett, leaning her elbows on the table, shook her fist at the child. "If you don't 'ang your father, Louisa, I'll come back, and I'll 'aunt yer by day, and by night, and I'll never leave yer."

"I'll be sure to 'ang 'im, mother."

"What shall you say to the peeler as comes and finds me?"

"'Oh, my poor mother! oh, my poor mother!'"

The child sprang off the sugar box, and she held her clasped hands up in front of her, and there were not only tears in her voice, there were tears in her eyes. As a piece of realistic acting, suggesting the agony of a child's heart-broken grief, it was perfect.

"And what shall you say to the kind gentleman as asks you 'ow I come to die?"

"'If you please, sir'"—the child dropped a curtsey—"father come into the room, and he locks the door, and 'e says to mother, "I'm going to do for you, you —. I've often said I would, and now I will." And mother says, "Oh, Bill, you wouldn't kill me!" And father says, "I would, by —! There's another woman I likes better than you, and she won't 'ave me unless I puts you away, so I'm going to do it." Then father takes something out of his pocket in a paper, and he puts it into a cup, and he puts some gin out of mother's bottle, and he holds the cup out to mother, and he says, "You drink this." And mother says, "Oh, Bill, you wouldn't poison me!" And father takes hold of mother and he drags her on to the ground, and he hits her in the face, and he takes 'er head on 'is arm, and he says, "Drink this, you —!" If you please, sir, I didn't see if mother drank it, father was 'tween me and 'er.'"

The child dropped another curtsey.

"And then the kind gentleman will say, 'What happened then, my little girl?'"

The prompting was from the mother; the child went on—

"'If you please, sir, mother begins coughing, sir, and she says, "What was it, Bill?"

"And father says, 'You would spit it out, you —, would you?' And he takes a knife out of his pocket, and he sticks it into mother's stomach. Oh, mother! mother! mother!"

The child put her hands up to her eyes, as if to veil from them some dreadful spectacle, and burst into an agony of childish lamentation, which would have melted the heart of a stoic. Her mother nodded approbation—approbation which was, in at least one sense, well merited.

"And if the kind gentleman asks you if ever you heard your father threaten to kill me, what shall you say then?"

"'If you please, sir'"—another curtsey—"'he was always a saying as 'ow 'e 'd do for 'er, and mother, she used to say to me, that, one of these days, she knew as 'ow 'e would kill 'er, too.'"

Another burst of lamentation, a little more modified than before—artistically. Mrs. Drewett had sat, nursing her leg, rocking herself backwards and forwards on the chair, watching the performance with critical satisfaction. It deserved watching. As a performance it would have done credit to what is often described, oddly enough, as the "regular" stage.

"That's right, Louisa, don't you overdo it. Not pitching it too strong, but just strong enough, is everythink. I never see nothing like you, Louisa, so quick, and so clever, and so good to your poor mother. We'll 'ang your father, you an' me between us—only mind you don't forget a morsel of what I've taught you."

"Not a morsel, mother. Don't you fear. I'll 'ang 'im, safe as 'ouses!"

"I don't fear—I trust you, my lovey. You 'ave another drop along o' me, my girl."

Mrs. Drewett tilted some more of the contents of the bottle into the cup. She had a good drink herself. The dregs she left for the child. The child enjoyed them. The mother took something, screwed up in a piece of paper, from the pocket of her dress.

"This is poison, my lovey—certain death. It's what your father's going to kill me with." She giggled, tipsily. "And this is a knife what I kep' back from that last lot of tools of 'is I pawned—the knife'll be enough to 'ang 'im. We'll tie 'im up atween us, you an' me, and we'll do the trick as soon as 'e comes 'ome."

The mother and the child sat drinking together, waiting and watching for the return of the husband and the father.

II. The Father

"Hollo, William, what are you doing here? You're looking down in the mouth." The speaker was Mr. Thomas Dunn. Mr. Drewett drew himself away from the wall, against which he was leaning, and looked at him. Mr. Drewett was a big, hairy man, slow to think, and, as a rule, also slow to speak. A stupid, blundering sort of fellow, who always seemed to need an effort at recollection to enable him to decide exactly where he was.

"I'm a thinking of how to kill someone. That's what I'm a doing of."

Mr. Dunn looked him up and down. Mr. Dunn knew his friend, and he saw that the man was troubled.

"If I was you I wouldn't think of nothing of the kind. That sort of thinking don't do anyone no good. What's up now, William?"

"You know that there lot of tools you chaps gived me?—she's pawned 'em."

"No!"

"She 'ave."

"I thought you said you wasn't going to take 'em home."

"More I didn't—leastways, not quite 'ome. I 'id 'em on top of a old cupboard, what's outside our door. She must 'ave 'eard me putting 'em away. Leastways, when I got up, they was gone, and 'er with 'em. As I come along the street I met 'er coming out o' Spratt's. She had the ticket in 'er 'and, and the money for my tools in 'er—pocket. I felt like killin' of 'er then. Only she set up such a screechin' all the people came a-hinterfering."

"She's a beauty!"

"I'll kill 'er yet. She's done for me, and now I'll do for 'er—for good and all."

"Don't you go talking like that—it ain't like you at all, William. You come in and have a pint with me. That'll liven you up—you wants livening."

They turned into the bar. There Mr. Drewett had a pint with Mr. Dunn. And there Mr. Drewett met another friend. When Mr. Dunn went off to his work Mr. Drewett, having no work to go to, and no tools to do it with if he had, stayed behind with this other friend, and had a pint with him. The liquor having loosened his tongue, he held forth on the subject of his grievances to the loungers in the bar. The recital so touched the hearts of his listeners that they sought to solace his afflictions with other "drains" of beer. The result of which was that he said things which he did not mean to say, and which he did not mean when he had said them, and which he never would have said had he retained possession of his sober senses. When a man, who is generally insufficiently fed, has fasted through the day, and who, besides, is nearly maddened by domestic troubles—when this man drinks a pint or two of four-ale, it affects him much more than it would an habitual drunkard.

As Mr. Dunn, returning homewards from his work, glanced in at the door, he found Mr. Drewett still where he had left him. Only the man was changed. He was leaning against a corner of the bar, his hands in his breeches pockets, his cap on the back of his head, muttering, over and over again, "I'll kill her! I'll kill her!" as if it was a lesson which he had learnt by heart. He was stupid with drink.

Mr. Dunn made short work of him. He went right into the bar, and he caught him by the arm.

"William, I'm ashamed of you. What's the good of your going on at your old woman if you yourself goes on like this? You just come straight home 'long o' me."

Mr. Drewett consented to be led home, docile as a child. The beer which he had drunk, taking effect upon an empty stomach, had acted as a narcotic; he seemed stupefied, more than half asleep. His brain, never remarkable for perspicuity, was in such a state of fuddle that, as he himself declared afterwards, he had no clear idea of what was really happening. To him, all that took place seemed to take place in the confusion of a dream.

Mr. Dunn piloted him to the door of the house which contained what Mr. Drewett called his home. There he left him. As Mr. Dunn pursued his solitary way he commented to himself—

"She'll drive him to drink, that'll be the end of it. She's a nice wife for a man to have. A sound flogging or two would do her good. If I had my way she 'd get 'em."

Meanwhile, Mr. Drewett, in a condition of desperate muddle, was staggering and floundering up the staircase to his "home."

III. The United Family

The woman was standing up, supporting herself, as best she could, upon her tottering legs, pointing, with both of her trembling hands outstretched, at the creatures which were born of her delirium. She shrank farther and farther away.

"There's lots of 'em, Louisa. There's one just jumped down upon your 'and. There's another creeping through a crack in the wall, ah—h!" she screeched. "They're a-coming at me! don't yer let 'em touch me! don't yer!"

The child hopped about like one possessed, straining every nerve to ward off from her mother the things which were not there, and all the time so serious—such a mistress of make-believe.

"All right, mother; I won't let 'em touch yer—don't yer be afraid!"

The woman's mood was changed. She crouched, her hand raised above her head, in an attitude of eager attention. She was listening.

"'Ush!" The child was still. "There's someone comin' up the stairs! It's him!—it's your father! Move yourself, my girl!"

She herself moved quickly to the table. She turned the contents of the paper packet, which still lay on the table, into the cup which was without a handle; she diluted it with gin from the black bottle, stirring the mixture with her finger. She was in a tremor of excitement.

"I'm a-going to 'ang 'im! I'm a-going to 'ang 'im! If I am to kill myself, I'll 'ang 'im, so 'elp me gawd, I will!" She shook her fist at the child. "And you, Louisa, your mother's a-going to kill 'erself to 'ang your father, and if you forgets a morsel of what I've learned yer, I'll come back from my grave to 'aunt yer!"

The child's eyes glistened. Unlike her mother, she was not excited. But it was obvious that she was interested.

"I won't forget a morsel. I'll 'ang 'im, mother; I swear to gawd I will!"

The woman held up in front of her the cup which contained the mixture.

"There's enough there to kill twenty women. I know what's what, though there's some as doesn't think it let alone a poor broken-down old thing like me. It'll snuff me out just like a candle; that it will!" Her voice rose to a scream. "Curse 'im, I 'ate 'im! I 'ate 'im! and I allays 'ave. 'E wanted to keep me from the drink, though 'e knowed it was the only comfort what I 'ad, and now I'll 'ang 'im and I'll be even with the —!"

The sentence was finished in a whirlwind of execrations. Someone was heard floundering about outside the door. The woman lowered her voice.

"There he is! Now, Louisa, mind you don't forget."

The child replied in a whisper, "I won't forget, mother."

"Now you're going to see some fun—'ollo!" Someone outside lurched against the door. "Sounds as if 'e 'd been 'aving a drop 'isself. That'll make it all the easier—'e never could carry 'is liquor like a man, and they allays 'angs a bloke what murders 'is wife when 'e's in drink." She giggled. The handle of the door was grasped from without. "Louisa, as soon as 'e's inside, you move yourself and turn the key; it'll make it look wuss for 'im—now don't you forget!"

"No, mother, I won't forget."

The door was opened, with sufficient awkwardness, to admit Mr. Drewett. So soon as he was in, the child, with impish quickness, snatching the door from his unsteady grasp, shut it with a bang and turned the key. He, evidently not comprehending the manoeuvre, lurched backwards against the wall. Having gained its friendly support, against the wall he stayed. The husband and the wife eyed each other—or, rather, the woman eyed her husband, while he, so to speak, endeavoured to obtain her focus. Mr. Drewett was not in a condition to see anything plainly.

The woman giggled, holding all the while the cup in her hand.

"So you're going to kill me, are you?"

"Yes," Mr. Drewett hiccupped; "I'm going to kill you."

"Oh, you are, are you? You 'ear what yer father says, Louisa? You mark 'is words."

"Yes, mother, I won't forget."

It was strange how quietly absorbed the child appeared to be, with all her faculties keenly alert—like an intelligent child listening to an absorbing story.

"Are yer going to kill me for another woman what yer likes better than me, are yer?"

"Yes"—another hiccup—"I'm going to kill yer."

The woman giggled again.

"You 'ear what yer father says, my girl? 'E's a-going to kill yer poor mother 'long of another woman what he likes better nor 'er. Are you a-listenin', Louisa?"

"Yes, mother, I'm a-listenin'."

"Well, my bloke, there's enough poison in that cup to kill twenty women, let alone one. Are yer goin' to make me drink it?"

"Yes." There was a repetition of the hiccup and of the monotonous refrain. "I'm going to kill yer."

"There yer are, then, make me drink it."

The woman held out the cup to the man with a leer. He took it, but, obviously mistaking the intention with which it had been proffered, advanced it towards his own lips. She snatched it from him with an oath. In doing so some of the contents was spilt. This inflaming her to wrath, she struck him savagely across the face. He merely looked at her with a fuddled stare.

"You—!" With the cup held once more in her own hand she suddenly broke into a series of ear-splitting yells, "'Elp! 'elp! 'elp! 'E's a-murdering me! 'E's a-killing me! 'Elp! 'elp! Mur-r-der-r-r!"

As if the noise which the woman made was not sufficient to awake the dead, the instant she slackened, the child burst into shrill childish lamentations.

"Oh, my poor mother! oh, my poor mother! Father's killin' my poor mother!"

When she paused the woman giggled. She had the cup close to her lips. She whispered—

"Now, Louisa, mind you don't forget!"

"No, mother, I won't forget."

"Good-bye, my girl!"

Draining, as she spoke, the contents of the cup to the dregs, she threw the cup from her so that it shivered into fragments on the floor, setting up, at the same time, a hullabaloo such as one might have thought no single pair of human lungs would have been capable of. Although it was impossible for him to avoid hearing her, it was plain that Mr. Drewett had not the faintest notion what the bother was about. As he was looking at her with hazy eyes, his wife leapt at him like a tiger-cat.

"'Elp! 'elp! 'elp!" she screamed. "'E's killin' me! My gawd! Mur-der!"

The child, rushing to the window, threw it open, and, leaning out into the street, caught up her mother's cry—

"Oh, my poor mother! Father's killin' mother!"

The woman bit and scratched and struck and kicked the man, and clutched at his hair, and sought to tear his clothes from off him, until even Mr. Drewett was roused from his heavy stupor, and began, in grim earnest, to struggle with her. Hither and thither they went, from side to side of the room. Coming within reach of the knife which lay upon the table, the woman snatched it up, sending the table crashing to the floor as she did so.

"He's stabbin' me! he's stabbin' me!" she screamed.

The child passed the cry on into the street.

"Oh, my poor mother! Father's stabbin' my mother!"

The woman plunged the knife into her own bosom, cutting herself with it wherever she could.

IV. The Orphan

When the door was broken open, and the crowd came streaming into the room, they found the woman in what was afterwards described as "a pool of blood," on the floor, with her husband's knife lying at her side. Mr. Drewett was standing near her, himself all drabbled with blood, his clothing in disorder, looking distraught and wild enough to have been guilty of a dozen murders. Apart from the wounds which she had received from the knife, the woman was convulsed with agony; the "mixture" was beginning already to take effect.

As the constable forced his way through the excited people, the child ran to him, her small clasped hands held up in front of her.

"Oh, my poor mother, sir! Father's killed my mother!"

She cried as if her little heart would break. Women cried themselves as they heard her. There and then William Drewett was haled, handcuffed, off to gaol.

Before night Mrs. Drewett was dead. As she herself had said, she had taken enough of the "mixture" to kill twenty women. Acting on such a constitution as hers, its effect was even unusually rapid. She gave testimony against her husband before the end. In what was almost her last convulsive agony, she called her daughter to her side. The child leaned over her. The mother gasped out a last maternal injunction—

"Louisa—mind—you—'ang—yer—father."

The child whispered words of comfort to her mother's soul.

"Don't you fear, mother; I'll 'ang 'im, safe as 'ouses." And Louisa did.

When William Drewett was standing his trial for the murder of his wife, the judge remarked, in the course of his summing-up—

"There are three pieces of evidence to which it is my duty to especially direct your attention. First, there is the testimony of the witness, Thomas Dunn, on the question of premeditation; then there is the testimony of the dead woman herself, which she gave when she knew that she was dying—a moment when even the ordinarily most loose-speaking persons realise the responsibilities which may be attached to the words which they are using; and, in the third place, there is the testimony of the child, of the prisoner's own daughter, Louisa. And, with reference to that evidence, I am bound to say that I cannot recall a case, within my own experience, of evidence being given, in a court of justice, by a child of such tender years, with greater clearness, which was more to the point, and which evinced a finer appreciation of the serious, and, indeed, in such a case as hers, the terrible responsibilities which are associated with the position of a witness. For my part, gentlemen of the jury, the evidence of the child— she is but the merest child—affected me strongly. And although in doing so I may seem to be travelling somewhat out of my province, I would express a hope that the case of the child, Louisa Drewett, may commend itself to the hearts of the charitable."

It did. Louisa Drewett became quite a heroine. Her portrait was in all the illustrated papers; her name was on myriads of tongues. Her career, in the future, is likely to present features of peculiar interest. It had a beginning of such promise!

William Drewett was found guilty, and, after the usual delay, with all the form which the law prescribes, was hanged by the neck till he was dead.

How he Passed!

I. Mr. Stanbrough's Dream

"EATON SQUARE, W.

"Dear Mr Tyrrel, I shall call on you tomorrow afternoon. It is of paramount importance that I should know, with absolute certainty, if Leonard will pass. I fear! I fear! But if you can only assure me that he will, you will earn the undying gratitude of yours sincerely,

"Violet Stanbrough."

"Well, my dear Lady Stanbrough, I can assure you, with absolute certainty, that he won't." So I told myself as I perused her ladyship's letter. "A young man comes to us who knows nothing, and who, while he continues here, insists on learning less, and then his fond mother expects us to precipitate him to the head of the pass list by some process of hankey-pankey, which, I imagine, is supposed to be known to crammers. No, my dear madam, had it not been for your very urgent solicitations, Young Hopeful would have been shown the door within four-and-twenty hours of his arrival. The Honourable Leonard Stanbrough is a pleasing combination of weakness and vice. I doubt if he could go straight if he tried to—and I don't think he's likely to try."

While mentally commenting on Lady Stanbrough's letter I had rung the bell. I told them to send young Stanbrough to me. A minute after he came. A tall, lanky, over-grown young man, with a lisp, an eyeglass, and an embryo moustache.

"Here is a letter which may perhaps interest you." I handed him his mother's note. "What answer am I to give her ladyship when she comes?"

He took up his position on the centre of the hearthrug with his back to the fire—he is one of the very few young gentlemen who have ventured to take up that position when closeted with me.

"Poor dear old girl!" he said. Then he paused.

"I admire the filial admiration which prompts you to make the remark, Mr. Stanbrough, but is that all you have to say?"

He had been surveying the ceiling with his eyeglass. Now he brought his eye-glass down to me.

"Oh, I shall pass!" he observed.

"Indeed? I am very glad to hear it. Especially as it happens to be news to me. May I ask what grounds you have for your assertion?"

"Oh, I had a dream!"

"A dream? I've no doubt you had a dream."

"Yes, I had a dream last night." ("Latht night," he said.)

"I venture to conjecture that it was late last night."

"Was rather late. Fact is, two or three of us had supper with some of the Frivolity girls, and I expect something they put into the drinks gave me a kind of nightmare, don't you know." I admired his assurance, if I admired nothing else. I have had pupils as to whose proceedings—out of doors—I have had the gravest doubts, but I do not remember one who was quite so frank as her ladyship's son. "I've a suspicion," he immediately added, "that I got beastly drunk."

"And it is because you were drunk, or because you had the nightmare, that you say you will pass?"

"Well, you see it was rather a funny kind of nightmare, don't you know."

"I expect it had its humorous side."

"I saw all the papers, don't you know."

"You saw what?"

"All the examination papers."

"The deuce, you did!"

I looked the speaker up and down. He appeared to be quite at his ease—vacuous as ever.

"It must have been a remarkable nightmare, Mr. Stanbrough."

"Ya-as!"

"May I ask you to let me understand exactly what it is you mean?"

"Certainly! With pleasure! Delighted! I saw all the examination papers, and I copied 'em."

"Copied them?"

"Copied 'em. Struck me as rather a sensible kind of thing to do, don't you know—for me."

"To what examination papers are you alluding, Mr. Stanbrough?"

"To the examination papers full of questions, don't you know, for the fellows to answer, don't you know."

"Do you mean to say that you saw those papers in a dream?"

"Kind of nightmare. Expect it was something in the drinks, don't you know."

"Are you jesting, Mr. Stanbrough?"

"Jesting! Good gracious, no!"

He seemed positively alarmed. I am bound to allow he was not of a humorous turn—as a rule.

"And you say you copied them?"

"Rather! What do you think? Sensible of me, wasn't it? Mind my smoking?"

"Not at all—if you feel you want it. You will soon cease to be my pupil, Mr. Stanbrough, and far be it from me to cast a gloom upon your latest hours. Can you describe this—nightmare?"

"I was in a room, don't you know, and the papers were brought, don't you know, and I copied 'em, don't you know."

"And was this in a waking nightmare?"

"Don't follow."

"Oh, yes, you do! Am I to understand that you have had a private view of the examination papers?"

"In a kind of nightmare, don't you know."

"Mr. Stanbrough is telling you about his nightmare, is he! Quite an interesting story, is it not?" Martin, my partner, said this as, unannounced, he entered the room. He had a bundle of papers in his hand. "Mr. Stanbrough has been telling the story to the whole world. He has gone farther—he has lent his copy of the papers to his friends. This is the copy, is it not?"

Martin held out the bundle of papers. Stanbrough immediately advanced. Before Martin suspected his purpose he had snatched them from him.

"Thanks. So they are."

"Mr. Stanbrough, you will immediately return me those papers."

Stanbrough had placed them in his breast pocket. He was buttoning his coat.

"Not today, old man. Call again tomorrow."

Martin turned to me. He never had taken to the Honourable Leonard. Even her ladyship's very liberal cheques had failed to soften the hardness of his heart.

"Mr. Tyrrel, Mr. Stanbrough appears to have obtained, by surreptitious means, a copy of the questions which are to be set in examination."

The Honourable Leonard interposed.

"Surreptitious," he said, "I suppose, means nightmare."

"Nightmare! Mr. Stanbrough, do you really propose to yourself to obtain the rank of an officer, and of a gentleman, by means of a fraud and of a lie?"

"I don't want to quarrel with you, old man, so I think I 'd better go. Funny chap you are, Martin, 'pon my word you are."

That was the way in which this promising young man addressed his tutor.

"Do you mean to tell me that you copied those papers which I just now held?"

"In a dream!"

"Then how comes it that the handwriting is so different from your usual hand?"

"Nightmare, don't you know. There was something in the drinks. But I don't want to row—really now."

The Honourable Leonard made for the door. I interposed.

"Excuse me, Mr. Stanbrough, but, at this point, the interview can hardly close. I am always unwilling to doubt the word of one of my pupils, but there are occasions on which faith becomes folly. If you have, by any means, become acquainted with the questions which are to be set in the examination it will be my duty to communicate with the authorities."

The Honourable Leonard never turned a hair. With complete nonchalance he resumed his position in the centre of the hearthrug. For a moment he stood in an attitude of listening. I thought he was turning my words over in what stood for his mind. I was mistaken.

"Here's my mother," he said.

He had keener ears than I. Almost before the words were spoken, without any act of preliminary notice, the door opened, and Lady Stanbrough came bursting in.

"Excuse me, Mr. Tyrrel, for my unceremonious entrance, but they told me I should find you up here, and Mr. Martin, and Leonard! 'I will show myself up,' I said. How are you, my dear boy?" She took the "dear boy's" hands in hers, and kissed him. The "dear boy" showed as many signs of reciprocity as if he had been a pillar-box.

"I hope, Mr. Tyrrel, that you have good news. So much depends upon it. I know that he is wild, but you are so clever. Now will he pass?"

"I am sorry to have to tell you, Lady Stanbrough, that, by fair means, he won't."

Her ladyship sank into a chair. A lace handkerchief was raised to her eyes.

"You wicked, wicked boy! I knew how it would be! Now you'll have to emigrate, or earn your living, or do some dreadful thing or other, because your father won't pay your debts—I'm sure he won't!"

The son did not seem much moved by his mother's sorrow. He kept his eye and ears fixed on the ceiling, as though all his interests were centred there.

"I am still more sorry to add," I continued, "that your son, knowing perfectly well that there is no possibility of his passing by fair means, has, I fear, resolved to resort to fraud."

"What do you mean?"

I turned to the candidate for military honours.

"Mr. Stanbrough, if you will hand me those papers which you have in your pocket the matter shall go no further."

"See you hanged!" replied the candidate.

"Leonard! What language you use! What is the matter now?"

"The matter is that Mr. Stanbrough has obtained an advance copy of the papers which are to be set in examination, and, for all I know, an advance copy of the answers too."

"What would be the use of that?" At another time her ladyship's innocence would have amused me.

"To be quite frank with you, Lady Stanbrough, I fear that Mr. Stanbrough intends to obtain the Queen's commission by means of fraud."

"Leonard! What are you doing? I wish you would be advised."

Young Hopeful brought his eye-glass down to me.

"This comes of a fellow telling his dreams," he said.

"Mr. Stanbrough, are you prepared to swear, in a court of justice, or, for the matter of that, in a court of honour, that you obtained a copy of those examination papers by means of a dream?"

"I am. I don't set up to be a parson, but I am not a liar."

His calmness rather staggered me.

"Do you mean to swear that that copy was not obtained by means of material agency?"

"Hanged if I know about material agency, because I don't know what material agency is. I don't set up to be a swell, don't you know; but I swear this. I swear that I had a dream last night. I dreamt that I was in a sort of room. A lot of the fellows were there. They gave us a lot of papers. I don't know what the other fellows did with theirs, but I copied mine—I do know that. When I woke up there were these papers on the table. I've got 'em in my pocket now, and if it's the same to you—or if it isn't!—I'll keep 'em there."

I exchanged glances with Martin. There was an air of greater earnestness about the speaker than I had ever observed in him before.

"This is a very extraordinary story which you tell us, Mr. Stanbrough."

"I don't know if it is or if it isn't; it's true."

"But," put in Martin, "you don't tell us how you came to know that those particular questions were the questions which are about to be set in examination."

"That's where it is—I don't know; but I'll chance that, anyhow. A fellow like me doesn't have a dream like that for nothing."

"Nor how it comes if, as you say, you copied them, that the copy is not in your writing."

"There you are again! Perhaps when a fellow writes in a dream his fist is altered."

"Perhaps," said his mother, when Martin and I were mute, "when you gentlemen have quite finished, you will tell me the meaning of it all."

"For that, Lady Stanbrough, I must refer you to your son."

"Come along, mother, let's cut it. I'll post you up as we go along—that is, if you'll drop me at the Giraffes."

"I wish you wouldn't go to that horrible club."

"Horrible!" On his face was a look of genuine surprise. "Why, it's full of pugilists! Good gracious, mother, how you talk!"

When they had gone—and we let them go, mother and son—with the papers in his pocket, Martin and I had a little discussion on the subject of Mr. Stanbrough's "dream."

"Did you look at the papers?" I asked.

"I glanced at them. I saw enough to be sure that they were never written by him. They looked to me as though they had been copied by a lawyer's clerk."

"Then you don't believe this story about a dream?" Martin hesitated—or I thought he did. "Don't you think his volunteering the tale was rather curious? Supposing he obtained them through any of the channels through which such things are to be obtained, it would have been at least more prudent to have kept the fact of their existence quiet."

"I think this." Martin's tone was dry. "I think that with the papers he won't pass. I know his mental capacity, and I doubt whether it will be possible to hammer the proper answers, even poll — parrot fashion, into his head."

"He might take a copy of the answers with him into the room."

"He might. But I shouldn't advise him to try. I don't think that even he is fool enough for that. My own opinion is that even with the aid of his 'dream' he won't pass."

But he did—pretty low down, but still he passed. Not as a pupil of ours, for we never saw him again after he departed with his mother. We did not claim him as one of our successes—perhaps that goes without the saying—but we did take the trouble to make sure that there had been no personation in the case. That he had been present there can be no doubt—his seat had not been occupied by an obliging friend.

I was in Piccadilly one night last May. It was rather late, the weather was not too fine, and I was hurrying along, when, as I was passing Sackville Street, a voice fell on my ear which seemed familiar. Turning I found myself face to face with Mr. Stanbrough. There was no mistaking him—and, on his part, there was no mistaking me. He was in evening dress. His Inverness, open in front, was thrown back upon his shoulders, and I could see by his face he had been drinking. At his side was another man. He, too, was in evening dress. He was tall and dark. He had—no one could see him without being struck by the fact at once—a pair of the most remarkable eyes I ever remember to have seen—quite as remarkable as any of those wonderful "orbs" which we read about in novels, and that is saying not a little.

"Hallo!" cried Stanbrough. "Here's old Tyrrel! Tyrrel, how do you do?" He turned to his companion. "Hook it! You won't get anything out of me."

His manner was particularly offensive. But the other man did not seem to notice it. He was regarding me with a smile.

"So this is Mr. Tyrrel, is it? The Mr. Tyrrel, I presume. Good-night."

Lifting his hat he sauntered away. Stanbrough stood glaring after him till he was lost in the crowd. Then he turned to me.

"Hallo, Tyrrel, I haven't seen you for an age. Sorry I can't stop now. Got an appointment, don't you know."

He hastened away, leaving me, in my turn, smiling. Since he had donned the epaulettes Mr. Stanbrough had evidently not improved either in manners or in morals. I pursued my way. I had not gone a dozen yards when someone touched me on the shoulder. It was the Honourable Leonard.

"I say, Tyrrel, if that brute Lansberg comes and tells you any lies about me, don't you believe him—he's the greatest liar living."

I was a little amused. The young gentleman was excited.

"I don't understand you, Mr. Stanbrough. I know no one of the name of Lansberg."

"That was Lansberg whom you saw speaking to me. He's a thief. If he comes to you I'd give 'em orders not to let him in. Keep him out in the street."

"I am obliged to you for your advice, Mr. Stanbrough, and for your information as to the character of your friend. Advice coming from such a quarter I cannot fail to value."

I left him there, staring after me with half-drunken eyes, as if in doubt as to the meaning of my words. For my part I had other and more important matter on my mind. Almost immediately after the chance encounter was forgotten. When, the next day, the servant brought me a card with the name of "Hermann Lansberg" on it, it recalled no associations, and it was only when the stranger was ushered into the room that I recognised in him the person whom I had seen with Mr. Stanbrough, and whom that gentleman had advised me to keep out in the street.

II. Mr. Lansberg s Explanation

Daylight revealed the fact that Mr. Lansberg was exceptionally good-looking, though his was a type of beauty for which I, personally, have no taste. He was too much of the "stage hero" sort of man for me.

Not only was he dressed like a gentleman, but he bore himself like one. And when he spoke, I discovered that he was possessed of that greatest of all charms—a musical voice.

"I had the pleasure of seeing Mr. Tyrrel for the first time last night." I bowed. I was remembering Mr. Stanbrough's words. I felt that the less I had to do with that young gentleman's acquaintances the better pleased I should be. "Mr. Stanbrough, an old friend of mine, was, I believe, an old pupil of yours." I bowed again. "Was Mr. Stanbrough a diligent pupil when with you?"

"I am unable to discuss Mr. Stanbrough with a stranger. May I ask what is your business with me, Mr. Lansberg? I am particularly engaged just now."

He shrugged his shoulders.

"I am sure that Mr. Tyrrel, whose reputation is known to the whole world, would not wish to connive at a fraud."

I did not like the fellow's tone. Although it was perfectly courteous, it yet conveyed a sneer.

"I do not understand you, Mr. Lansberg. And, as I said just now, I am particularly engaged."

"Very well, Mr. Tyrrel." He had been taking his ease in an armchair. Now he rose. "Far be it from me to intrude upon your pressing labours. I would merely mention that I am about to inform the Horse Guards that Mr. Stanbrough, at that time your pupil, obtained his commission by means of a fraud, of which fraud you were aware. Good-day."

"Mr. Lansberg!"

He had reached the door, but he turned again.

"Mr. Tyrrel?"

I at once decided that the fellow's object was blackmail. I resolved to foil him there, at any rate.

"You are, of course, at liberty to take any steps you please. I would merely advise you to be careful how you mention our name."

"My dear sir, I shall not mention your name. I have too much respect for your character—and my own. I shall merely repeat Mr. Stanbrough's words."

"And what are they?"

"He tells me that he obtained an advance copy of the examination papers. He says that you were well aware of the fact, that he himself was your informant. In my note to the Horse Guards I shall mention this, adding, that I have no doubt that Mr. Stanbrough's story, so far as it relates to your having a guilty knowledge of his fraud, will be found, upon inquiry, to be unreliable."

A pretty scoundrel the fellow was. And nice fools Martin and I had been! If such a story got about it might entail our ruin.

"Did Mr. Stanbrough, among his other confidences, tell you how he came into the possession of the papers?"

"Ah, now you are coming to business!" The fellow sat down again, and nursed his leg. "Now you are coming to the point!"

"He told us that he obtained them by means of a dream."

"Is it possible, then, that you were aware that they were in his possession! But, of course, you at once communicated with the authorities."

"May I ask you, Mr. Lansberg, to tell me frankly what is the purpose of your presence here?"

"I think you have guessed already." I suppose I started, for he immediately added, "No, Mr. Tyrrel, for once your prevision is at fault, you have guessed wrong. I might make a pleasant little income out of the information which I hold, but, at present, such is not my intention. I will be frank with you—my intention is to be frank. My purpose here is—to smash my friend!"

"Explain yourself, Mr. Lansberg."

"Does not the situation explain itself? My reasons—my reasons are my own. I say to myself I have information which will—smash him! If I use that information it will look a little awkward. I say, therefore, that you shall use that information, and I will smash him—by deputy!"

"Really, Mr. Lansberg, you propose to us a very pleasant office."

"If you decline, then I shall use the information and smash you both together. Because I can prove that you were aware that an advance copy of the papers was in his possession."

"He told us that he obtained them by means of a dream."

"Pooh, my dear sir, pooh! Was that any reason why you shouldn't have communicated with the authorities? You were well acquainted with his character, and the tale was quite incredible."

I indulged in a few moments' consideration before I answered.

"Mr. Lansberg, you are a stranger to me, and I have no wish to pry into the reasons which actuate your conduct. That conduct is rather a matter for your consideration than for mine. But with reference to this matter of Mr. Stanbrough, I would remark that he swore, solemnly, in our presence, and in the presence of his mother, that he obtained those papers by means of a dream."

"But you don't seem to see my point. Even supposing that what he said was true, was that a reason why you should not communicate with the authorities? Don't you see that your own story looks a little ugly?" I did see it—but I did not tell him so. Our decision to forbear, which had been made in haste, promised to give us cause to repent at leisure. The man went on: "I am sure you will see that the disclosure would come more gracefully from you. And I am so sure, that I will be quite frank with you— why should I not? I know that those papers were not obtained by means of a dream."

"How do you know?"

"Because they were obtained through me."

"Mr. Lansberg!"

"So you see I ought to know."

The man's assurance was superb. I perceived that he and his friend made a capital pair.

"Do you mean to tell me that you obtained those papers for Mr. Stanbrough, and that then you come and threaten us?"

"No threat intended—none at all. I suggest what I think you will find, upon reflection, to be the wisest course of action. And in doing so I place, at your service, further information—gratuitously."

"This, I suppose, is a conspiracy between you two?"

"It was. It is now going to be a conspiracy between us too—you and I."

I have seen equally impudent men—in farces! Never out of them!

"If it is not trespassing unduly upon your courtesy, Mr. Lansberg, may I ask how you obtained these papers for your friend?"

"My dear Mr. Tyrrel, I shall be delighted to make of you a confidant, although I fear that you will find my story almost as incredible as Mr. Stanbrough's. I may preface it with the observation that the matter was managed in such a manner that it would be impossible to take action against me, even on my own confession."

"I have no doubt, from what I have seen of you in this short interview, that the matter was managed with exquisite skill."

"Not only skill, Mr. Tyrrel, not only skill! Something higher than skill. Science—knowledge—power. I obtained those papers by means of hypnotic force."

"By means of what?"

"Hypnotic force."

I am no great believer in the current craze for undeveloped forces. And as for some of the marvels of so-called "hypnotism," I fear that I should have to see—and test!—before I believed. But I perceived at a glance that here was a man who was as likely as any other man to work such wonders. There is something in the magic of the eye, and this man undoubtedly possessed it. I never saw such eyes. I myself found it difficult to meet his glances. And his manner, voice, and general deportment conveyed suggestions of latent forces, which, to me, were wholly disagreeable. Still I began, in spite of myself, to take an interest in the scamp—interest which was of a peculiar speculative kind.

"I am afraid you will have to make yourself clearer, Mr. Lansberg, before I am able to grasp your meaning."

He made himself quite clear.

"Ever since I was a mere boy I have been conscious of the hypnotic power. I think I might even manage to hypnotise you."

"You might find it more difficult than you perhaps imagine."

"I think not. I think that I might succeed—in time."

"Suppose we return to the subject in hand."

I did not like his tone at all!

"To the subject of the papers! With pleasure. My first acquaintance with Mr. Stanbrough was a hypnotic one."

"How do you mean?"

"It was—why should I conceal it?—at a bar. I hypnotised him then and there. Under my direction he drank a bottle of brandy—neat." I looked at the man who could own to such things he might have been talking about the weather. "Of course, that sealed our friendship then and there."

"It would!"

"You mean that with a young man of Mr. Stanbrough's stamp it would—how well you know him! I found that my young friend had several engaging qualities. He was a knave who pretended to be a fool."

"You make no pretensions to folly, Mr. Lansberg?"

"Not any. I am a knave—self-confessed! Why should I conceal it from a kindred soul?" I had provoked it—yet I winced. This fellow was, in his way, magnificent. "In course of time my friend found himself in a singularly difficult position. He had failed before. If he failed again he might expect no money from his father. It would be as easy for him to swallow the monument as to pass the examination in the ordinary way. As friends should do, we put our heads together. What was to be done? Personation was played out. Besides, in this case there were circumstances which made the thing impossible. Could we get a glance at the examination papers? Easier said than done. Curiously enough, I happened to know the proof-reader whose duty it was to revise those very examination papers as they came from the press. He was a man of the very highest character. I invited him one day to dine with me in the privacy of my own apartments. I asked him, casually, whether supposing some scamp were to offer a large sum of money for a rough copy of those particular papers, it would be possible to obtain one. He explained, to my entire satisfaction, that it would not. At that particular printing-office things were so managed that it was made plain, even to me, that it would be quite impossible. As I was realising this, an idea occurred to me which amounted to an actual inspiration. Was it not possible to obtain from my friend the proof-reader, in another way, what I wanted? And that without his knowledge? I tried, and succeeded. I waited till the table was cleared. Then I hypnotised him—a better subject I never had! I told him to write down what he remembered of the questions which were to be set in examination. He wrote them all down. Then I told him to write the answers. He was a man of great erudition, and it occurred to me that, even with the questions, we might be at a loss to find the answers. He answered them, every one! Then I gathered the papers together. I put them in my pocket. I withdrew the influence. And—we had a glass of wine."

"Really, Mr. Lansberg, I don't know which story is the more remarkable, yours or Mr. Stanbrough's. Do you mean that that man—that proof-reader was unconscious of what it was he was doing?"

"As unconscious as—"

What comparison he was going to make I cannot say. Before the words had passed his lips, he rose from his seat. He turned to the door. It was opened and Mr. Stanbrough came in! Lansberg threw up his arms with a gesture of burlesque melodrama.

"My prophetic soul! My uncle!"

"I thought I should find you here, you hound!" This was Mr. Stanbrough's greeting to his friend. He took no notice of me. Continuing, his hat upon his head, he stood and glared at Mr. Lansberg. In return, Mr. Lansberg smiled at him. "I called at your place. They told me where you'd gone—there's someone there can tell me things as well as you. I spotted your little game." He turned to me. "Didn't I warn you against him? What lie has he been telling now?"

Mr. Stanbrough was revealing himself in a new light. Hitherto, so far as it had come within my range of observation, the chief feature in his character had been his imbecility. Now he seemed to be rather more of a brute than a fool. I hardly knew in which guise I liked him least. Mr. Lansberg answered the inquiry which he had addressed to me.

"I have been telling Mr. Tyrrel,. my dear Leonard, the whole story of your—dream."

"It's a lie! He can hatch up any story!"

Advancing, Mr. Lansberg went and stood close up to his friend. He fixed his eyes upon his face.

"It is no lie."

"I say it is a lie! Don't you touch me! Don't you try to do anything to me, because you can't!" Again the Honourable Leonard turned to me. "He is a mesmerist, this fellow. He has been playing the devil with me for years. I have fed and clothed him. He has mesmerised me, and then, when I didn't know what I was doing, he has made me do what he liked; he has robbed me of thousands! But he can't do it any longer; I have got beyond him; he has lost his power; he will never mesmerise me again—never! So because I won't shell up to keep him going he says he'll smash me. But he can't! He tells nothing but lies! Liar!"

He turned upon Lansberg with the yelp of an angry cur. Their faces were within a few inches of each other. One, however, was as cool as the other was hot.

"My dear Leonard, up to a certain point you tell the truth. I have found you useful as a subject now and then. It is true that of late I seemed to have lost my power, but when you say that I shall never mesmerise you again, you are mistaken. I will mesmerise you now! Stand still! and look at me!"

The change in the man was wonderful. He seemed to have increased in stature; his eyes dilated; his voice was altered. The Honourable Leonard gazed at him as though he exercised the proverbial fascination of the snake.

"Lansberg!" he gasped. "Lansberg!"

That gentleman said nothing. He seemed to be using his utmost exertions to produce a certain result. Raising his hands he made some passes before the victim's face. The Honourable Leonard visibly shuddered; Mr. Lansberg's efforts relaxed. Smiling, he turned to me.

"It is true, my power is going! I never had to use so much force before. Still, our young friend was wrong. He has been mesmerised again, you see! You will now behold that little scene with the proof-reader performed before your eyes. Leonard, dear boy, sit down."

He pointed to my writing-table. Without a word or sign of remonstrance Mr. Stanbrough crossed the room and seated himself in front of it.

"You remember the circumstances connected with those examination papers?"

"Yes."

"Write down a short and correct account of all that happened, and sign it! Nothing extenuate, nor aught set down in malice! I believe I have the quotation right?" He turned to me with what he doubtless intended should be a charming smile. "Commence, dear boy."

Mr. Stanbrough took a pen, drew a sheet of paper towards him, and began to write. I could scarcely believe that the scene which was being enacted before me was not a little performance got up for my special benefit.

"Do you mean to tell me, Mr. Lansberg, that Mr. Stanbrough is in a state of complete unconsciousness?"

"Ask him yourself."

I spoke to him. "Mr. Stanbrough!" There was no reply.

"Shake him up."

I went and laid my hand upon the young man's shoulder. "Mr. Stanbrough!" I repeated. Still no reply. I was startled when I saw his face; the muscles seemed fixed and rigid. All expression had disappeared— he never had much, but what little he ordinarily had was gone; the eyes were staring wide open.

"Won't he answer you?" Mr. Lansberg took out a penknife; he opened a tiny blade. "Stick this into him." I shrank away. "Then if you won't, I will." Stooping, he thrust the blade of the knife into the young man's thigh. The Honourable Leonard never winced; he continued to write with a calmness which, under the circumstances, I found unpleasant. "Will that suffice? or shall I pin his hand to the table? I'm sure he won't object."

I declined his offer. I was content to see the scene played through. Whether the unconsciousness was real or fictitious, experiments of that kind did not commend themselves to me. Lansberg kept up a running commentary of remarks while Stanbrough continued writing. I was still. At last the Honourable Leonard laid down his pen. Wheeling round in his chair he observed to Lansberg, very much as we might imagine that an automaton would make a similar observation—

"I have finished."

"Thanks, dear Leonard, thanks." Mr. Lansberg took up the paper on which he had been writing. He read it carefully through. "Your composition does you credit, Leonard—and your accuracy! Now I think you may come back again."

With his hands he made some fresh passes before the victim's face. Again Mr. Stanbrough shuddered. He rose from the chair. He seemed dazed.

"What's the matter? Where am I? I—I thought —" His glance fell on Mr. Lansberg. "Curse you! Have you been at me again?"

"Yes, my dear Leonard, I have been at you again. And you, too, have been at it again. Allow me, Mr. Tyrrel, to hand you Leonard's own, true, faithful, and particular account of how he became possessed of those examination papers. Now I really think that I must say good-day. I have only one remark to make to Mr. Tyrrel. It is this: if, within four-and-twenty hours, you do not tell the story—I shall. Tell any story you please, only—tell one. I feel sure that you will perceive, upon reflection, that it would be better for all of us if the initiative were taken by you."

"And I, Mr. Lansberg, have but one remark to make upon my side. If you imagine that I should take advantage of a confession obtained by such means as those which I have witnessed, you are mistaken. That is all."

I tore the paper into pieces. The pieces I threw into the grate.

"As to that, Mr. Tyrrel—as you please. Good-day! Good-day, dear Leonard."

Bowing low, he left the room. Mr. Stanbrough and I stared at the door through which he had vanished.

"Good riddance to a thief," remarked his friend.

"If, Mr. Stanbrough, you follow my advice, you—will follow the thief."

He followed him. His exit was certainly the less graceful of the two.

"Now what is to be done?"

Later in the day I related all the circumstances to Martin. It was to him I put the question.

"First of all," he said, "where are those pieces of paper. I mean the paper which purports to be Mr. Stanbrough's confession."

"They are in the grate."

"Then we must get them out of the grate."

I happened to have had no fire in my room that day. The fireplace was littered with waste paper. Martin, going down on his knees, went carefully through the litter. I assisted him. We recovered the pieces. Then we pasted them together on a large sheet of foolscap—much as a child might piece together the different fragments of a puzzle.

"I don't understand, Martin, your motive in doing this. I said that I would make no use of the contents of this paper."

"Then if you won't, I shall. In dealing with rogues honest men must make use of whatever tools they find to hand. There, now, I think, we have the whole of it." Martin read it carefully through. Then he handed it to me. "Read it, and tell me what you think of it."

It was unmistakably in Mr. Stanbrough's writing. It was short and to the point. The wording was clear and simple. It stated that the first suggestion as to the papers had come from Mr. Stanbrough. He had asked his friend to obtain for him a copy. Lansberg, as he had told me, procured one from the proof-reader while the man was in a state of mesmeric trance—a copy both of the questions and the answers. Stanbrough learned the answers off by heart. When, however, it came to the actual examination he had already forgotten the greater part of them. The result was that he only just scraped through. All this was stated, quite plainly and frankly, in his own scrawling caligraphy. At the bottom of the document was affixed his name.

"A nice young man!" said Martin. "A very nice young man! And how he lied to us—like truth!"

"The question is, what is the best thing for us to do?"

"We will go, with this document in our hands, to Mr. Stanbrough, and we will advise him to send in his papers to the Horse Guards—to himself take the initiative, and resign. I have no doubt that we shall be able to put the matter in such a way that, before the interview is concluded, he will see his way to act on our advice."

We went to him then. Mr. Stanbrough was out. We left a note, intimating that we should return in the morning at eleven, and strongly advising him to be there to receive us. This time he was in. He received us with scant courtesy. He remained seated. A bottle of brandy, with a tumbler half filled with the raw spirit, was on the table at his side.

"So it's you, is it? I hoped I'd seen the last of you."

He added some choice expletives, which I need not particularly describe. Martin was suave in the extreme.

"We will not unnecessarily detain you, Mr. Stanbrough, but will come to the point at once. We are here to advise you, for reasons with which you are aware, to immediately resign the commission which you hold!"

"I thought it was something of the kind! But it's too late! I've resigned already!"

"I am afraid that we shall require to have proof of that!"

"Proof! Curse you! What has it to do with you? Look at that!"

He tossed a note across the table. Martin picked it up, and read it. When he had read it he passed it to me. It was a request from Mr. Stanbrough, not too nicely worded, for his papers. I returned it to Martin.

Folding it up, he placed it in the pocket of his coat.

"I will see that it is duly despatched," he said.

Mr. Stanbrough made no comment upon the action. He swore "at large." Early as was the hour, the young man had already been drinking freely.

"Don't think I'm doing it because of you. You couldn't have done anything to make me! I've done it on my own hook. I've come a cracker! Stonebroke! Owe everyone! And these fellows here are a lot of card sharpers! They think I'm a fool—but I ain't!"

"I think that when you say that we could do nothing that you forget the existence of a certain paper."

"Tyrrel tore it up. He said he wouldn't use it."

"But I have pieced it together again, and I will use it."

Mr. Stanbrough was visibly disconcerted. He drank the brandy which was in the tumbler.

"Use it, and be damned!"

"And surely you are forgetting such a factor as Mr. Hermann Lansberg."

"Lansberg!—Lansberg's dead!"

"Dead?"

I suppose our startled faces tickled him. He laughed uproariously.

"Yes, dead! dead! I daresay you think I murdered him. I should have liked to, but I didn't—curse him! But he's dead! And a jolly good job too!"

Whether he was speaking the truth I cannot say. Possibly he was. We asked no questions. We should have received no trustworthy answer if we had. We have heard nothing of Mr. Lansberg since. Frankly, we have not troubled ourselves to inquire if he is dead or living. Very shortly after, we saw that the resignation of the Honourable Leonard Stanbrough was gazetted.

Richard Bernard Heldmann was born on 12th October 1857, in St Johns Wood, North London, to parents Joseph Heldmann and Emma Marsh.

Shortly after his birth his father became ensnared in a bankruptcy proceedings which enforced the abandonment of a career as a merchant for that of a schoolmaster at a school in Hammersmith, West London.

By his early 20's the young Heldmann, showing a talent for writing, began publishing fiction. In 1880, he began to publish works of boys' school and adventure stories for the myriad magazine publications all eager for good well-written content. The most important of these was Union Jack, one of the better quality boys' weekly magazine associated with the popular authors G. A. Henty and W.H.G. Kingston.

Heldmann was promoted to co-editor in October 1882, but his association with the publication ended suddenly in June 1883. After this, Heldmann published no further fiction under that name.

The reason at the time was not immediately apparent but in April 1884 Heldmann was sentenced to 18 months of hard labour for issuing a series of cheques, all forged, in France and Britain the year before.

In order to be well away from the scandal and damage this had caused to his reputation Heldmann adopted a pseudonym on his release from jail. Shortly thereafter the name 'Richard Marsh' began to appear in the literary periodicals. The use of his mother's maiden name seems both a release from the criminal record now associated with his given name and a lifeline to a fresh beginning.

A stroke of very good fortune arrived when his novel The Beetle was published in 1897. There had been more than a few previous publications of his works but The Beetle would turn out to be his greatest commercial success and added some much-needed gravitas to his literary reputation. The story concerns a mysterious oriental person who follows a British politician to London, and then wreaks havoc with his powers of hypnosis and shape-shifting. The Beetle has some similar aspects to certain other novels of the period, including those such as Bram Stoker's Dracula, George du Maurier's Trilby, and Sax Rohmer's many Fu Manchu novels. Like Dracula, and also the sensation novels written by Wilkie Collins and others during the 1860s, The Beetle is narrated from the various viewpoints of multiple characters to create suspense. The novel is also layered with many themes and issues of the Victorian era including women's rights, unemployment, urban poverty, radical politics, homosexuality, science, and Britain's imperial adventures, particularly in regard to Egypt and the Sudan. The Beetle sold out upon its initial print run and thereafter sold well for the next several decades. After Marsh's early death the novel's story was made into a film and adapted for the London stage, both in the 1920's.

It should also be noted that in the year of its first publication it outsold Dracula, then also in its first year of publication. In hindsight a remarkable achievement.

Marsh was a prolific writer and wrote almost 80 volumes of fiction as well as many short stories, across several genres from horror and crime to romance and humour.

However, at horror he was particularly adept. Works such as The Goddess: A Demon (1900), in which an Indian sacrificial idol comes to life with murderous resolve, and The Joss: A Reversion (1901), whose central premise is that of an Englishman who transforms himself into a hideous oriental idol are prime examples.

An important element of many of Marsh's novels is the investigation of the mystery. Several of his novels are centered on the crime and its subsequent detection. In the novel Philip Bennion's Death (1897) a bachelor is discovered dead the day after discussing Thomas De Quincey's essay on murder as a fine art, and his neighbour and friend begin efforts to solve his death. In The Datchet Diamonds (1898) a young man who has lost a fortune on the stock market mistakenly swaps bags with a diamond thief, and then find himself pursued by both the thieves and police. In A Spoiler of Men (1905), Marsh puts together crime and science-fiction; the gentleman-criminal villain renders people slaves to his will by a chemical injection.

As with many authors success with popular fiction was never quite enough. He also wanted to be regarded as a serious author. His novel A Second Coming (1900) imagines Christ's return to an early-20th century London and is his most well-handled attempt in that pursuit.

His prolific output of short stories ensured his being published in a plethora of magazines including Household Words, Cornhill Magazine, The Strand Magazine, and Belgravia, as well as in a number of short story book collections. These collections; The Seen and the Unseen (1900), Marvels and Mysteries (1900), Both Sides of the Veil (1901) and Between the Dark and the Daylight (1902) all feature an eclectic mix of humour, crime, romance and the occult.

He also published several serial short stories. Here he was able to develop characters whose adventures could be related in discrete stories across numerous editions of a magazine. An example is Mr. Pugh and Mr. Tress of Curios (1898). They are rival collectors between whom pass a series of bizarre and disturbing objects—poisoned rings, pipes which seem to come to life, a phonograph record on which a murdered woman seems to speak from the dead, and the severed hand of a 13th-century aristocrat.

During his career he sometimes came up with characters or stories ahead of their time. His character Miss Judith Lee, a young teacher of deaf pupils whose lip-reading ability involves her with mysteries that she solves by acting as a detective was very pro-active in this regard.

Richard Marsh died from heart disease in Haywards Heath in Sussex on 9th August 1915.

Several of his novels were published posthumously.

Richard Marsh – A Concise Bibliography

As Bernard Heldmann
Boxall School: A Tale of Schoolboy Life (1881)
Dorrincourt [Union Jack, April-September 1881]

Expelled: Being the Story of a Young Gentleman (1882)
Daintree (1883)

As Richard Marsh
Capturing a Convict (Strand Magazine 1893)
The Devil's Diamond (1893)
The Mahatma's Pupil (1893)
The Strange Wooing of Mary Bowler (1895)
Mrs Musgrave—and her Husband (1895)
The Mystery of Philip Bennion's Death (1897)
The Crime and the Criminal (1897)
The Duke and the Damsel (1897)
The Beetle: A Mystery (1897)
The House of Mystery (1898)
Under One Cover: Eleven Stories by S. Baring-Gould, Richard Marsh, Ernest G. Henham, Fergus Hume,
Andrew Merry and A. St John Adcock (1898)
Curios: Some Strange Adventures of Two Bachelors (1898)
Tom Ossington's Ghost (1898)
The Datchet Diamonds (1898)
The Woman with One Hand and Mr Ely's Engagement (1899)
In Full Cry (1899)
Frivolities: Especially Addressed to Those Who Are Tired of Being Serious (1899)
The Purse Which Was Found
For One Night Only
Returning a Verdict
The Chancellor's Ward
A Honeymoon Trip
The Burglar's Blunder
Ninepence
A Battlefield Up-to-date
Mr. Harland's Pupils
A Burglar Alarm
A Lesson in Sculling
Outside
The Chase of the Ruby (1900)
An Aristocratic Detective (1900)
A Hero of Romance (1900)
The Seen and the Unseen (1900)
The Goddess: A Demon (1900)
Ada Vernham, Actress (1900)
A Second Coming (1900)
Marvels and Mysteries (1900)
The Long Arm of Coincidence
The Mask
An Experience
Pourquoipas
By Suggestion
A Silent Witness

To Be Used Against Him
The Words of a Little Child
How He Passed!
The Joss: A Reversion (1901)
Both Sides of the Veil (1901)
Amusement Only (1901)
The Twickenham Peerage (1902)
Between the Dark and the Daylight (1902)
The Adventures of Augustus Short: Things Which I Have Done for Others and Wish I Hadn't (1902)
A Metamorphosis (1903)
The Death Whistle (1903)
The Magnetic Girl (1903)
Miss Arnott's Marriage (1904)
Garnered (1904)
A Duel (1904)
A Spoiler of Men (1905)
The Marquis of Putney (1905)
The Confessions of a Young Lady (1905)
Under One Flag (1906)
In the Service of Love (1906)
The Garden of Mystery (1906)
A Woman Perfected (1907)
The Romance of a Maid of Honour (1907)
The Girl and the Miracle (1907)
The Surprising Husband (1908)
The Coward behind the Curtain (1908)
That Master of Ours (1908)
A Royal Indiscretion (1909)
The Interrupted Kiss (1909)
The Girl in the Blue Dress (1909)
The Lovely Mrs Blake (1910)
Live Men's Shoes (1910)
The Twin Sisters (1911)
A Drama of the Telephone (1911)
Violet Forster's Lover (1912)
Sam Briggs: His Book (1912)
Judith Lee: Some Pages from her Life (1912)
The Master of Deception (1913)
Justice—Suspended (1913)
If It Please You (1913)
The Woman in the Car (1914)
Molly's Husband (1914)
Margot—and her Judges (1914)
The Man with Nine Lives (1915)
Love in Fetters (1915)
His Love or his Life (1915)
The Flying Girl (1915)
Violet Forster's Lover (1916)

The Adventures of Judith Lee (1916)
Sam Briggs, V.C. (1916)
Coming of Age (1916)
The Great Temptation (1916)
The Deacon's Daughter (1917)
On the Jury (1918)
Orders to Marry ([1918)
Outwitted (1919)
Apron-Strings (1920)

Periodicals

For Debt, Windsor Magazine (January 1902)
Returning a Verdict, Cornhill Magazine (January 1896)
The Lost Duchess, Cornhill Magazine (January 1895)
Mrs Riddles Daughter, All the Year Round (17 March 1894)
An Episcopal Scandal, Cornhill Magazine (February 1894)
A Rubber or Two, All the Year Round (16 September 1893)
A First Night, Cornhill Magazine (April 1893)
The Mystery of Philip Bennion's Death, Household Words (3/10/17/24/31 December 1892)
The Princess Margaretta, Household Words (3 December 1892)
The Puzzle, Cornhill Magazine (November 1892)
A Victim to Art, All the Year Round (2 July 1892)
The Burglar's Blunder, Derby Mercury (24 June 1891)
Pourquoipas, All the Year Round (9/16 May 1891)
The Pipe, Cornhill Magazine (March 1891)
When Greek Joined Greek, Household Words (6 September 1890)
His First Experiment, Cornhill Magazine (September 1890)
"Mignonette", All the Year Round (9 August 1890)
The Long Arm of Coincidence, Household Words (24 May 1890)
The Match of the Season, Cornhill Magazine (May 1890)
A Set of Chessmen, Cornhill Magazine (April 1890)
A Dream of Diamonds, Household Words (7 December 1889)
My Uncle's Flirtation, Household Words (16 November 1889)
"Em", Household Words (2 November 1889)
The Barnes Mystery: An Adventure of Judith Lee, Strand Magazine (October 1916)
"Scandalous!", Strand Magazine (August 1916)
What Fell on her Hat, Strand Magazine (April 1916)
The Adventures of Sam Briggs: On the Film, Strand Magazine (March 1916)
A Set of Chessmen, Cassell's Magazine of Fiction and Popular Literature (Dec 1915)
Sam Briggs Becomes a Soldier: A Fighting Man, Strand Magazine (December 1915)
Sam Briggs Becomes a Soldier: On the Way Home, Strand Magazine (November 1915)
Sam Briggs Becomes a Soldier: An Official Mistake, Strand Magazine (October 1915)
Sam Briggs Becomes a Soldier: In their Own Gas, Strand Magazine (September 1915)
Sam Briggs Becomes a Soldier: Sanctuary, Strand Magazine (August 1915)
Sam Briggs Becomes a Soldier: In the Nick of Time, Strand Magazine (July 1915)

Sam Briggs Becomes a Soldier: A Night Surprise for the Germans, Strand Magazine (June 1915)

Sam Briggs Becomes a Soldier: In the Trenches, Strand Magazine (May 1915)

Sam Briggs Becomes a Soldier: Baptism of Fire, Strand Magazine (April 1915)

Sam Briggs Becomes a Soldier: Two Stripes, Strand Magazine (March 1915)

Life in the King's New Army: Jack Carpenter's True Story, VI: Career for our Boys, Daily Mail (27 February 1915)

Life in the King's New Army: Jack Carpenter's True Story, V: The Tailor and the Man, Daily Mail (26 February 1915)

Life in the King's New Army: Jack Carpenter's True Story, IV: Hutments', Daily Mail (25 February 1915)

Life in the King's New Army: Jack Carpenter's True Story, III: First-Rate Fighting Men', Daily Mail (24 February 1915)

Life in the King's New Army: Jack Carpenter's True Story, II: The Berwick Borderers, Daily Mail (23 February 1915)

Life in the King's New Army: Jack Carpenter's True Story, I: Crossed Swords, Daily Mail (22 February 1915)

Sam Briggs Becomes a Soldier: A Man in the Making, Strand Magazine (February 1915)

Sam Briggs Becomes a Soldier: Sam Briggs Becomes a Soldier, Strand Magazine (January 1915)

The Amazing Visitor, Strand Magazine (December 1914)

Looping the Loop: An Adventure of Sam Briggs, Strand Magazine (August 1914)

The Torch, Strand Magazine (October 1913)

"Gaiety" Abroad, Strand Magazine (September 1913), 274-82

A Self-Appointed Guardian, English Illustrated Magazine (August 1913)

For the Cause, Strand Magazine (April 1913)

The Adventures of Judith Lee: The Affair of the Montagu Diamonds, Strand Magazine (February 1913)

The Adventures of Judith Lee: Mandragora, Strand Magazine (August 1912)

The Adventures of Judith Lee: "8 Elm Grove—Back Entrance", Strand Magazine (July 1912)

The Adventures of Judith Lee: The Restaurant Napolitain, Strand Magazine (June 1912)

The Adventures of Judith Lee: Uncle Jack, Strand Magazine (May 1912)

The Adventures of Judith Lee: Was It by Chance Only? Strand Magazine (April 1912)

The Adventures of Judith Lee: Isolda, Strand Magazine (March 1912)

The Adventures of Judith Lee: "Auld Lang Syne", Strand Magazine (January 1912)

The Adventures of Judith Lee: The Miracle, Strand Magazine (December 1911)

The Adventures of Judith Lee: Matched

The Burglary in Berkeley Square, Pearson's Magazine (December 1908)

The River of Light, Strand Magazine (December 1908)

The Girl in the Light Blue Dress, Strand Magazine (October 1908)

O'Rourke of the Saucy Sixth, Grand Magazine (June 1908)

The Adventures of Sam Briggs: The Limerick, Strand Magazine (February 1908)

The Adventures of Sam Briggs: The Star of Romance, Strand Magazine (July 1907)

The Adventures of Sam Briggs: A Social Evening, Strand Magazine (April 1907)

My Best Story and Why I Think So No. 21: The Strange Occurrences in Canterstone Gaol, Grand Magazine (October 1906)

The Adventures of Sam Briggs: That Hansom, Strand Magazine (May 1906)

The Adventures of Sam Briggs: Her Fourth, Strand Magazine (December 1905)

The Adventures of Sam Briggs: A Modest Half-Crown, Strand Magazine (November 1905)

The Adventures of Sam Briggs: The Gift Horse, Strand Magazine (March 1905)

My Wedding Day, Strand Magazine (January 1905)

The Adventures of Sam Briggs: The Girl on the Sands, Strand Magazine (October 1904)

The Parson, the Soldier, and the Child, London Magazine (November 1903)
The Girl and the Boy, London Magazine (October 1903)
By Whose Hand? New Short Novel by Richard Marsh, Answers (1 August – 31 October 1903)
A Girl Who Couldn't, Strand Magazine (January 1903)
The Kit-Bag, Windsor Magazine, 17 (January 1903), 298-309
Their Reasons: Two Hitherto Unreported Conversations, House Annual (1902)
At Large: Being the Strange Perils and Experiences of George Otway, Suspect, Answers (12 July - 27 December 1902)
The Handwriting, Strand Magazine (June 1902)
La Haute Finance, Windsor Magazine (March 1902)
A Wonderful Girl, Strand Magazine (March 1902)
Skittles, English Illustrated Magazine, (February/March 1902)
Breaking the Ice, Strand Magazine (February 1902)
My Aunt's Excursion, Windsor Magazine (January 1902)
The Haunted Chair: The Story of a Strange Mystery, Harmsworth London Magazine (January 1902)
Miss Donne's Great Gamble, Strand Magazine (November 1901)
The Man in the Glass Cage; or The Strange Story of the Twickenham Peerage, Manchester Times, (6 September – 27 December 1901
The Adventures of Augustus Short: Things Which I Have Done for Others, and Wish I Hadn't: The Address Which I Gave for Rudman, Cassell's Magazine (November 1901)
The Adventures of Augustus Short: Things Which I Have Done for Others, and Wish I Hadn't: Jones's Love Affair, Cassell's Magazine (October 1901)
The Adventures of Augustus Short: Things Which I Have Done for Others, and Wish I Hadn't: The Duel I Fought of Jarvis, Cassell's Magazine (September 1901)
The Adventures of Augustus Short: Things Which I Have Done for Others, and Wish I Hadn't: Griffin's Offspring, Cassell's Magazine (August 1901)
The Adventures of Augustus Short: Things Which I Have Done for Others, and Wish I Hadn't: McCulloch's Shoes, Cassell's Magazine (July 1901)
The Adventures of Augustus Short: Things Which I Have Done for Others, and Wish I Hadn't: The Fitzroy-Jenkinsons' Rooms, Cassell's Magazine (June 1901)
Staggers, Windsor Magazine (April 1901)
How I Drove a Motor Car for Randal, Strand Magazine (April 1901)
The Disappearance of Mrs Macrecham: The Amazing Story of a Strange Cat, Harmsworth Monthly Pictorial Magazine (March 1901)
The Irregularity of the Juryman, Strand Magazine (December 1900)
The Strange Fortune of Pollie Blythe: The Story of a Chinese "God", Manchester Times (12 October 1900 – 8 February 1901)
Pugh's Poisoned Ring, Harmsworth Monthly Pictorial Magazine (October 1900)
Willyum, Penny Illustrated Paper and Illustrated Times, (26 May 1900)
Willyum, Hampshire Telegraph and Naval Chronicle (26 May 1900)
The Goddess: A Demon, Manchester Times (12 January – 30 March 1900)
The Stolen Treaty, Manchester Times (27 October 1899)
For One Night Only, Answers (8 April 1899)
In Full Cry, Manchester Times (3 March – 9 June 1899)
The Colonel's Cane, Cassell's Magazine (February 1899)
The Burglary at Azalea Villa, Manchester Times, (13 January 1899)
The Burglary at Azalea Villa, Newcastle Weekly Courant (14 January 1899)
Our Christmas Burglar, Answers (17 December 1898)

Something to his Advantage, Manchester Times (7 October – 4 November 1898)
A Lesson in Sculling, Newcastle Weekly Courant (October 1898)
That Five Hundred Pound Price, Harmsworth Monthly Pictorial Magazine (September 1898)
The Chancellor's Ward, Harmsworth Monthly Pictorial Magazine (August 1898)
The Ossington Mystery, Ipswich Journal (1 April – 17 June 1898)
The Duchess of Datchet's Diamonds, New Zealand Graphic and Ladies' Journal (New Zealand) (7 May – 25 June 1898)
The Peril of Paul Lessingham: The Story of a Haunted Man, Answers (13 March – 19 June 1897)
The Purse Which Was Found, Answers (17 April 1897)
The Rector and the Curate, Answers (19 December 1896)
An Illustration of Modern Science, Pall Mall Magazine (November 1896)
A Battlefield Up-to-Date, Idler Magazine (August 1896)
Twins, Idler Magazine (January 1896)
Lady Wishaw's Hand, Leeds Mercury (January 1895)
Young George, St Nicholas (March 1894)
Exchange Is Robbery, Idler Magazine (December 1893 - January 1894)
The Tipster: An Impossible Story, Home Chimes (December 1893)
The Influence of Women, Home Chimes (November 1893)
By Deputy: A Reminiscence of Travel, Home Chimes (October 1893)
Rivals, Home Chimes (September 1893)
Capturing a Convict, Strand Magazine (August 1893)
A Burglar Alarm, Home Chimes (June 1893)
Music Halls and Theatres, Home Chimes (March 1893)
A Strange Bride, Manchester Times (6/13 January 1893)
The Mask, Gentleman's Magazine (December 1892)
A Vision of the Night, Strand Magazine (December 1892)
Nelly, Home Chimes (November 1892)
A Prophet: A Story, New England Magazine (October - November 1892)
Mr Harland's Pupils, Home Chimes (August 1892)
The Brothers in Grey, Home Chimes (April 1892)
The Half-Back, Derby Mercury (March 1892)
The Half-Back, Home Chimes (February 1892)
The Violin, Home Chimes (December 1891)
The Short Story, Home Chimes (August 1891)
Magical Music, Gentleman's Magazine (May 1891)
A Honeymoon Trip, Home Chimes (April 1891)
Mitwaterstraand, Time (September 1890)
A Pack of Cards, Longman's Magazine (August 1890)
The Burglar's Blunder, Ladies' Journal (Canada) (1 July 1890)
The Strange Occurrences in Canterstone Jail, Blackwood's Edinburgh Magazine (June 1890)
A Substitute: The Story of My Last Cricket-Match, Longman's Magazine (June 1890)
The Burglar's Blunder, Gentleman's Magazine (May 1890)
A Silent Witness, Belgravia (October 1889)
A Bed for the Night, Belgravia (Summer 1889)
Payment for a Life, Belgravia (Summer 1888)

www.ingramcontent.com/pod-product-compliance
Lightning Source LLC
Chambersburg PA
CBHW051252170626
46809CB00004B/1611